Secrets and Dreams

A great scream suddenly pierced the snowy, calm, deserted world and after our initial shock we realized that this was Luce having the best kind of fun. She had just gone careering down a very steep slope on a plastic bag, and landed in a heap at the bottom. There was no one else in sight and it really felt as though we'd arrived in the most glorious winter wonderland. Bracken Valley was a vast dip, sunk into an area of very high ground. Within this dip there were little separate hills and valleys carved out, and it was down one of these little hills that Luce had just pelted.

"Doesn't it hurt your bottom?" I asked with my usual anxiety.

"No, it's such thickly padded snow, and I've got a thickly padded bottom too," she replied brightly.

Also in the Cafe Club series by Ann Bryant

The CAFÉ Special Club

Secrets and Dreams

Ann Bryant

Hippo

Scholastic Children's Books,
Commonwealth House, 1–19 New Oxford Street,
London WC1A 1NU, UK
a division of Scholastic Ltd
London ~ New York ~ Toronto ~ Sydney ~ Auckland

First published in the UK by Scholastic Ltd, 1998

Copyright © Ann Bryant, 1998

ISBN 0 590 11329 1

Typeset by Rowland Phototypesetting Ltd, Bury St Edmunds, Suffolk
Printed by Cox & Wyman Ltd, Reading, Berks.

Chapter 1

Luce

Hi! It's me – Luce. I'm sorry, but I can't talk right now. I'm too excited to talk. In fact, I'm too excited to do anything, so I'm just standing here with my mouth open, too gobsmacked even to worry that a passing fly might think my mouth is an interesting-looking cave worthy of exploration. And the reason for this statue-like behaviour on my part is because I am holding a letter – sorry, I know I'm squeaking, it's the excitement – which says . . . hang on a sec, I've just got to tell Mum.

"Mum! Mum! Guess what? You know that competition I entered?"

I rushed into the kitchen at four hundred and fifty-six miles per hour and noticed that Mum, whose attention was on the pastry she was rolling out, raised an eyebrow. I wondered what she'd do if I broke through the sound barrier one day. Probably bat an eyelid, or something equally dramatic.

"I won it! Look! I won it! I can only take one person with me and it's Jaimini. Sorry Mum, it would have been you, but the twins need you and so does Terry. I'm going to tell her."

I tossed the letter on to the table and tore out of the back door. Mum was wiping her hands on her apron. Grown-ups! Talk about calm. I'm glad I'm not a grown-up: I couldn't cope with all that self-control. I'd have to keep going off to private places where I could pull faces, or stick my bottom out one way, my nose out the other way, and say "Nur-nur" to the wall.

Just wait till Jaimini heard my news. If truth be known, she didn't actually deserve to be my chosen companion for this holiday, after all the grief she'd given me when I'd entered the competition in the first place. But I could forgive her now that everything had turned out so incredibly well, and she *was* my best friend, after all. I mean, what are best friends for if not to come with you on mega-fantastic trips to New York?

Something rather uncomfortable was happening to me as I half walked and half ran to Jaimini's house. I couldn't think what it was at first, because I was too wrapped up in my thoughts, but then I realized. Thoughts weren't very good protection from the icy blasts of cold air that were bringing me out in goosebumps all over. A big woolly jacket would have been a better bet but, of course, being me, I didn't think about anything practical like that.

Maybe I'd better tell you exactly who "me" is. My name is Lucy Edmunson and I'm thirteen years old. I live with my mum, my stepdad, Terry, and my twin brothers, aged eight, who are called Tim and Leo and who are, incidentally, pains of the first order. I go to school at Cableden Comp, where I'm in year eight. I have five really good friends who are also all thirteen and go to the same school. My best friend out of these five is Jaimini Riva, which you pronounce *Jay-m-nee Reever*. Jaimini lives with her mum, who is white, and her dad, who is black, which explains why Jaimini has the best skin it's possible to have, in my opinion – coffee-coloured. My own skin is rather pale and freckly.

While we're at it I may as well list the other contrasts between Jaimes and me. She's got long, straight shiny black hair that she's taken to wearing in lots of little plaits. I've got thick bundles of curly auburny-blonde hair. She's got black eyes (and I don't mean that someone's whacked her) and I've got boring bluey-greeny-grey eyes. The biggest contrast of all is that Jaimini, out of all our group, is the brainy one, whereas I've been labelled the crazy one. Great, isn't it?

As I seem to be on the theme of contrasts I'll tell you next about Andy Sorrell, short for Agnes (pronounced Ann-yes), who is half French. Her mum is French and her dad is English, but he works in France most of the time. Andy is the smallest of us all, with very short dark hair and dark eyes. Andy is the daring one. Her best friend is Leah Bryan, who has long blonde hair and a pale complexion and generally makes you sick because she's so talented and modest. She's the musician, you see. She plays the violin and the piano. She's also chief worrier, despite the fact that she never really has anything to worry about – not compared to me, anyway. Nobody has quite got my brilliant ability to get into scrapes on a daily basis. Leah lives with her mum and dad and her big sister, Kim, who's fifteen. By the way, Andy has got a baby brother, Sebastien, who's just one, I think.

Tash, short for Natasha Johnston, is the peacemaker. Tash is everybody's friend and it's impossible not to like her. She's got an older brother, Danny, who's going out with Leah's sister, Kim, and a little sister called Peta who is just three and is very entertaining. Their mum is a single parent. Tash's hair is quite short and dark brown, and her face is very striking, especially when she smiles, which she does a lot. Her best friend is Fen, short for Fenella Brooks.

In a way I should have started with Fen as she's a sort of kingpin in our group, being the ambitious one. She came up with this terrific idea to get us all jobs working in her Aunt Jan's cafe. We take turns working there each day after school, then one of us works on Saturday. We rotate every week so we all get a turn to do a Saturday, which means longer hours, so more money. Fen lives with her mum and dad and her two sisters, Rachel, aged nine, and Emmy, aged five. So that's the Cafe Club for you. And now, back to the plot!

"Luce, you must be totally and utterly stark staring mad!" was Jaimini's greeting as she opened her front door and beheld this shivering, probably red-nosed (because my nose always goes red in the cold) apparition. "Quick, come inside. There's nothing the matter, is there?" She suddenly looked really concerned.

"Only something mind-blowingly wonderful," I told her with a secretive smile.

"Come on, spill."

We went up to Jaimini's bedroom, which is one of the most atmospheric rooms I've ever been in. I decided that this would be a suitable backdrop for my amazing news. Once we had gloriously sunk into Jaimes's squidgily comfortable bean bags, I told her.

"I've only gone and won that competition that you said I hadn't a cat in hell's chance of winning!" It was brilliant watching the expression on her face. She was waiting for me to carry on, but I'd stunned her with my great news. "You remember what the first prize is, don't you?"

"Trip to New York?" she croaked, in her I-cannot-believe-this-is-for-real voice.

4

"Exactly," I told her, grinning triumphantly. "And despite the fact that you openly mocked me for even bothering to enter the competition in the first place, I have decided to forgive you, and even let you be my chosen companion for the week!"

"The week! A whole week! When? Oh, what if I can't go?!"

The expression on Jaimini's face had to be seen to be believed. It was such a mixture of desperation in case her parents said she couldn't go, and excitement at the thought of going.

"Let's tell the others," I said.

"Yeah. Oh, maybe not."

"Why not? It's the news of the century and I want to spread it."

"Yeah, but they can't come."

"They'll still be happy for us."

"OK, but don't go on about it too much. I mean, don't rub it in, you know."

"Let's start with Tash," I said, picking up the phone.

"Hello," said Tash.

"Hi, Tash, it's Luce. Guess what?"

"What?"

"I've only won a trip to New York!" Stunned silence at the other end of the line. "Good, isn't it?"

"That's absolutely brilliant, Luce. When did you hear?"

"This morning. It came in the post. I've just told Jaimini. It's a trip for two, you see."

"Oh, that's wonderful news, Luce. I bet Jaimes is thrilled, isn't she?"

"Yeah, just a bit," I giggled. "She's lying on the floor in shock."

Tash laughed like mad when I said that, then I heard her mum calling her and she said she'd got to go.

"Phone Leah next," suggested Jaimini. "I still can't believe it, you know," she added, hugging her knees.

"Me neither," I lied, because actually I was already on the plane in my mind.

"Hi, Kim. Is Leah there? It's Luce."

"Hi, Luce. I'll just get her."

A minute later Leah was on the phone, and she gave me the same sort of reaction that Tash had. You could always rely on Tash and Leah to be enthusiastic and really happy for you. I knew it wouldn't be quite the same with Fen and Andy. I don't know why exactly. It's not that they wouldn't be happy for us, just that they don't show their feelings in quite the same way. We tried Fen next but there was no reply.

"They're out Christmas shopping," Jaimini told me after I'd let it ring nineteen times.

"Oh great, thanks for telling me, Jaimes."

"I only just remembered. Fen said yesterday that the whole family were going on a big expedition to try and do the whole lot in one hit."

"Right, let's try Andy then. Do *you* want to try Andy, Jaimes?"

"No, it's *your* news. You do it. Andy'll be thrilled, you'll see."

"Hello? Hello, Andy?" I covered the mouthpiece and spoke to Jaimes. "It sounds like I've got hold of a death-watch beetle."

"What!"

"Tons of tapping. Oh, hang on, what's this? Hello, Andy?"

6

"A-da-da-da-da-brbrbrbr."

"It's Sebastien." I giggled. "He's talking gobbledegook."

"Here, let me talk to him," said Jaimini, grabbing the phone from me.

"Why? I didn't know you spoke fluent gobbledegook."

"Hello Sebastien," said Jaimes, with a silly motherly look on her face, as though Sebastien could see her, "Can you get Andy?" There was a pause. "Get Andy," Jaimini tried again, cutting her sentence down to the basics, but still using her encouraging singsong voice. "Get Andy, Sebastien," she repeated, sounding a bit sharper. "Andy, Andy Andy!" she finished, rather exasperatedly.

"What's he saying?" I inquired in a loud whisper, because it was very frustrating not being able to hear both sides of the conversation.

"A-dee-a-dee-a-dee-a-dee," Jaimini informed me, without changing her expression.

"That's interesting," I said sarcastically. "It's important to keep up with what's happening on the stock exchange."

"Well *you* try getting hold of Andy then," she said, thrusting the phone back at me rather impatiently.

"Hello," I said into the mouthpiece in a bored voice.

"Hi, Luce, sorry about that."

"Oh, hi, Andy." Jaimini looked suitably hacked off, I noted with satisfaction. "I was just ringing to tell you the great news I got this morning."

"Yeah?"

"I won that competition I entered. First prize is a trip to New York for two. I'm taking Jaimes."

"Great. That's great, Luce." So why didn't her tone match her words? From her voice you'd think I'd just told her I'd found a five pound note – good, but not the news of the century. "When did you hear?" She was the second person to ask me that.

"This morning. In the post."

"What does your mum think?"

"She thinks it's great . . . well, she hasn't actually said. I didn't really give her the chance – you know how it is. I just came straight out to tell Jaimes."

After I'd put down the phone I felt myself sliding gently from cloud forty-nine to about cloud twenty-two. "Do you want to see the letter, Jaimes?"

"What letter?"

"Telling me the good news, of course."

"Yeah OK, then we can talk dates with your mum."

"Yeah, then we can talk dates with *your* mum!"

We clasped each other's hands like little kids, and started jumping up and down and giggling. It was going to be so great.

"Hi, Mum!" I called, as Jaimini and I crashed into our kitchen about half an hour later. Mum was nowhere to be seen, but there were plenty of signs to show that she wasn't far away, like things sizzling and simmering in pans. And sure enough, five seconds later she pelted into the kitchen and stopped dead at the sight of me, as though I had been magically transformed into a leopard since she'd last seen me.

"Luce, sit down."

"Why?"

"Because I've got some bad news for you."

"What? *What*? I don't want to sit down. What's happened? It's not something that's going to stop me going to New York with Jaimes, is it? It had better not be. Anything but that. Anything."

"You misread the letter, Luce. You didn't win first prize,

you won *a* prize. You won ten pounds to be precise. I'm sorry darling, I really am. Don't look like that. That's right, sit down. I'll put the kettle on. Look, I'm sorry. I wouldn't have wished this upon you for the world, but I've read it and reread it to be sure that I'm right. And I am. You simply haven't won first prize."

Her words just kept ringing in my ears. "You simply haven't won first prize." "You simply haven't won first prize." "You simply—"

"She's right," said Jaimini in a very soft voice. She had picked up the letter and was holding it tightly with both hands, scanning every line quickly. "She's right."

Why did everybody keep repeating everything?

"Say something, Luce. Please don't look like that, darling. It's not the end of the world."

"It is," I managed to mumble.

"No, it isn't. We'll organize something else to make up for it. How about that?"

Mum was crouching down in front of my chair, holding my hands and trying to look at my bowed face. I wouldn't let her. I felt like being as miserable as I could for as long as I could. I felt like a kid of six. Life was *so* unfair.

"What about Auntie Alice?"

"What about Auntie Alice?"

"You could stay with her, and Jaimini could go too. She'd love to have you. She's always asking me when you can go up there."

"It's not quite the same, is it?" I said, raising my head briefly so she could have the benefit of my most witheringly sarcastic expression.

"It's better than nothing, Luce," said Jaimini, in a gentle voice. She was acting more like a mother than a friend, which irritated me. Why wasn't she slumped in a chair with her spirits crushed, like me?

"I'm not sure that it *is* better than nothing, actually," I replied, still in my sullen voice as I scanned the letter and saw immediately that it was obvious I'd only won ten pounds. In fact, I'd no idea how I could have got it so badly wrong. I must need my eyes testing.

"What about if all six of you go up there?" said Mum, leaping up with a big, triumphant grin on her face, as though she knew she'd just pressed the right button and I was on the point of jumping up and hugging her for thinking of such a wonderful plan. Nothing was further from the truth.

"Has she moved into a castle or something?" I asked flatly, as a picture of Auntie Alice's little semi-detached flashed through my mind.

"That's a point," admitted Mum. "I was forgetting about that. Well, maybe just you and Jaimini, then."

At that point the phone rang. Mum went out to answer it. She came back into the kitchen a couple of minutes later, and handed the phone to me.

"It's Andy. I've told her. And I mentioned about Auntie Alice, too."

"Hi."

"Hi, Luce. Sorry."

Andy rarely wasted words.

"Me too."

I often waste words, but today I didn't feel like talking.

"Maybe it's fate."

"What do you mean?"

"Maybe you were meant to be staying with your Auntie Alice because something really exciting is going to happen while you're there."

10

When she said that, I felt the tiniest stirring of excitement. It was just enough to pull me out of my gloom. I straightened up in the chair.

"What did you phone for, anyway?"

"I had the feeling that something had gone wrong."

"Since when have you been psychic?"

"It's not that. It was just that alarm bells rang when you said that you hadn't actually had any reaction from your mum. I thought, Oh no, has Luce got this right?"

"You haven't got much faith in me, have you?" I asked indignantly.

She didn't reply, and no wonder, really. After all, she'd been spot on, hadn't she?

"Why don't you come round for a while, Andy?" I suggested impulsively.

About half an hour later, all six of us were together in my room, because Andy had alerted the others and they'd all decided to come round to cheer me up. We were making each other laugh by coming out with more and more ridiculous suggestions as to how we could all manage to sleep at Auntie Alice's. Fen's latest idea was that I should sleep in the bath, Andy, being the littlest, in the dog basket, she and Tash in the spare room in proper beds (typical), Jaimini on the settee and Leah on the piano!

"I've got a better idea," Andy said. "What about a tent in her garden?"

"You're joking, we'd freeze to death," said Leah. "I'll stick with the piano."

At that moment Mum came in with a twinkling look in her eye. "I've organized for you all to go," she said, triumphantly.

"All of us? How did you manage that?" I asked a bit

11

doubtfully, with Andy's suggestion still ringing in my ears.

"I decided to phone Alice and see what she said. Apparently, there's a small guest house in the next street from Alice's, and the owners are away for three weeks over the Christmas and New Year period. Alice's daughter, Jules, is house- and dog-sitting while they're away, and she says it won't be any inconvenience at all to have the six of you staying there. In fact, she could use the company."

"Oh, brilliant!" said Leah.

"When?" I asked, beginning to warm to the idea.

"The day after Boxing Day, for a week."

Immediately we all looked at one another and each held our breath. I think we all had the same thought in our heads – what if one of us couldn't go because of family arrangements?

"Do you want me to phone round your parents?" Mum asked after a moment, and the answer from all the other five was a definite "yes, please". We all know from experience that parents are much more likely to say yes to requests from other parents. All the same, we waited nervously in my bedroom till Mum came back, then we scrutinized her face for any sign of a problem.

"*Your* mum wasn't too sure, Jaimini, and neither was your dad, Andy, because of the fact that they don't know Jules, and they were naturally worried about how much of a free rein you might be getting. It's understandable."

"Oh great," muttered Andy darkly. Jaimini just looked miserable.

"But don't worry. I phoned Helen next [that's Tash's mum] and she very kindly offered to come up too, and keep an eye on you all, if that would make people's parents feel more comfortable with the idea."

"Oh, your mum's so brilliant," Fen said, hugging Tash impulsively.

"And what did Dad say when you told him that Helen would be coming too?" asked Andy.

"All of your parents are perfectly happy with the arrangements now, so it's settled," said Mum, beaming round at us all.

I found myself beaming round at everyone too, and it was lovely to see how happy they all looked – well, all except Tash, that is.

"What's the matter, Tash? You get on fine with your mum," said Fen.

"I presume that Peta will be joining the party," Tash said, looking most unimpressed.

"Oh yeah! Great!" the rest of us all said immediately, because Peta really makes us laugh.

"Great!" agreed Tash, rolling her eyes, but she was smiling, because underneath her my-little-sister's-a-pain act, she actually adores Peta.

Chapter 2

Leah

I love Christmas. I always have done. I don't know which I love more, Christmas Eve or Christmas Day. The excitement and the build-up are almost better than Christmas itself! And this year seems more exciting than ever because of the thought of going off to Derbyshire with my friends. I've never met Luce's Auntie Alice, and Luce has only ever spoken to her on the phone. She's Terry's older sister and she's got three daughters. Jules is twenty-three. I'm not sure how old the others are. It's going to be great because we'll all be together. We've been on holiday together once before, but that was to stay with our French penfriends and so we were split up. This time we'll all be under the same roof. And I'm glad that out of all the parents it's Helen who's coming with us, because she's so lovely and sweet and understanding about everything.

On Christmas Eve in our family we all put our presents under a big rug. You see, we've got a window seat in the sitting room and we stuff the presents under there and then cover them all up with the rug. Mum and Dad have kept up this tradition ever since we were little and, a few years ago, when they asked us gently whether or not we felt that we'd grown out of it, both Kim and I were devastated and said that we absolutely loved it and that we'd never grow out of it. When I'm married with my own children I'm going to do the same thing.

Kim and I don't have stockings any more, but we all give a lot of presents to each other, and any other presents that come into the house get put in a high cupboard in Mum and Dad's room, and then brought down and hidden under the rug on Christmas Eve. This means that we all share everyone's pleasure at opening every single present. Mum's brother, Eddy, always comes for Christmas, along with his wife, Laura. They've got three children: Celia, who's eleven, Beth, who's seven, and Tom, who's six. I'm very fond of the younger two, but I just don't get on with Celia. I feel horrible not liking her, but I can't help it. She's kind of sly.

I don't know how she does it, but she always manages to be the one who gets the piece of Christmas pudding with the pound coin in it, and whatever game we're playing, she cheats to make sure she wins. She must be very clever to manage to do it so subtly. In fact, it's so very subtle that sometimes I think I must be wrong and that it's just coincidence or skill or both that Celia always wins. When I'm thinking like that, I really hate myself for ever doubting my poor cousin, but then something else will happen and I catch a look of triumph on her face that makes me start disliking her all over again. If I'm honest, having Celia to stay is the only thing that slightly spoils Christmas for me, but it's only very slightly, because I love Uncle Eddy and Auntie Laura and the two little ones.

On Christmas Eve at about seven o'clock I was helping Mum and Kim in the kitchen. We were making punch for the next day. At the same time, we were getting ahead with preparations for Christmas lunch so that we'd have as little as possible to do the next day. Dad was putting crackers on the Christmas tree – or so I thought. When I went in to have a look at the tree, which I'd done about twenty times in the last half hour because I love the sight of it with all the little lights twinkling away, I found Dad sitting on the settee writing on little bits of paper.

"No looking. I'm writing the clues for the treasure hunt."

"Oh brilliant. I'd forgotten about that."

This was a fairly new custom. In fact, last year was the first time we'd tried it, and it was such a success that Dad had obviously decided to try it again. Dad is absolutely excellent at writing clues. He's very inventive and imaginative, even though he's quite a scatterbrain and a very old-fashioned sort of father these days. He's the only person I've ever come across who smokes a pipe. He also loves playing chess. Andy gets on really well with Dad. I think that's because he's such a contrast to her own father. Andy loves coming to our house because she says it's so cosy and hasn't got any hint of bright, crisp modern life, except perhaps for the kitchen.

"Are you doing two hunts or just one?" I asked Dad, because last year he'd made up one hunt for me and Celia and another easier one for Beth and Tom. Kim, Mum and Dad, along with Eddy and Laura, had followed us round, seeming perfectly content to watch us without joining in.

"I'm going to attempt a second one after this," Dad said thoughtfully. I decided to leave him to it. He was puffing on his pipe and narrowing his eyes, partly out of concentration and partly because of the smoke. This is exactly how I visualize Dad when we're not together. He's such a dear old dad.

It took me ages to get to sleep on Christmas Eve. In the end, I went into Kim's room and then I felt even more wide awake because we chatted about all sorts of things. Kim and I are quite close. People say we look very similar but I think she's much prettier than me. She's so slim. Her hair is straight like mine, only a little darker, and it hangs better than mine does. Also, she's very natural. She hardly ever wears any make-up. There are loads of boys who'd like to go out with her but she's not interested. She only likes Tash's brother, Danny.

"We're not going to be able to get up in the morning if we don't go to sleep pretty soon," said Kim, after about half an hour of talking.

"*I* will. I've never ever had a problem with getting up on Christmas Day. I can't wait to watch everybody opening their presents from me."

"You always say that, Lee. Do you really prefer to watch other people opening presents than opening your own?"

"Yes. I know it makes me sound like the most sick-making person in the world, and I wouldn't admit it to anyone but you and Andy, but I really do love to watch other people opening presents, and if the present's from me and the other person really likes it, it makes it even better."

"But don't you just love opening your own presents and seeing what you've got?"

"Oh yes, course I do. I can't wait to see what Mum and Dad have got me. It feels really funny having no idea at all."

It was the first year that I could remember when I hadn't specially asked for anything in particular. I'd just said, "Surprise me!" and Mum and Dad had been very secretive indeed about something in their bedroom, banning me from going in there for the past three weeks. It wasn't like Mum to get excited and have secrets. She's a much more down-to-earth sort of person than that. She and Dad are like chalk and cheese, really. Mum appears to be the one who runs the house and makes the decisions, while Dad potters along in the background, but I've noticed once or twice that actually, if you watch carefully, it's really Dad who's making the major decisions, only he does it very quietly. Dear old Dad.

"What's Andy getting you this year?"

"I've no idea. I'd forgotten all about Andy's present. Last year she left my present with Dad when she played chess with him. Maybe she's done the same thing this year. She certainly hasn't given anything to me. What's Danny getting for you?"

"I can't be sure, but I've got the feeling it might be a bag. You know what he's like. He'd never be able to think of something all on his own, so I've helped him by dropping little hints about what I really wished I had. I started in October, to give him plenty of time to catch on and then do something about it."

Kim and I promptly collapsed into giggles when she said that, because it suddenly seemed really wicked of her to have Danny so much in her power that she could even control what he got her for Christmas, without him being the slightest bit aware that he hadn't thought of it for himself!

I didn't remember what day it was straight away when I woke up the following morning, but when I did, I absolutely shot out of bed, then looked at my watch. Eight o'clock! That was pretty late for me to be waking up on Christmas Day. I rushed into Kim's room to find her asleep, so I called out to her to wake up then rushed into Mum and Dad's room. It was empty. "Happy Christmas, you two!" I called out as I ran downstairs.

"Happy Christmas, you one!" said Dad happily.

"I was just making you and Kim a cup of tea," said Mum. "Dad and I couldn't believe it when we realized we were up before you two."

"We couldn't get to sleep last night, and we talked for ages and ages," I explained as I extracted one of the cups Mum was holding. "I'll take this up to Kim."

When we'd all had breakfast and made a lovely coal fire in the sitting room we settled down to the magic present-opening ceremony. We all sat on the floor and Dad made it last as long as possible. Kim loved the two tops I'd bought her. I knew she would, because one of her friends had described to me what Kim had been admiring in a catalogue, and I'd bought something that I thought was practically identical.

I guessed rightly that Mum and Dad would save their present to me till the very end, and after a while I began to get worried in case I didn't like whatever it was and I had to pretend I did. They might realize that I was faking happiness, which would be terrible. When my mind started working along these lines I gave myself a severe talking-to because I'm such a terrible worrier, and Christmas is the one time when I really should not be worrying about anything. Anyway, I guessed that Kim probably knew what Mum and Dad had got me, and she wouldn't let them buy me something that I wouldn't like.

"And finally," said Dad, flinging the big blanket out of the way to reveal one last present, "this is for you, Leah, with love from Mum and myself."

They were both beaming broadly as I opened the package with trembling fingers. It was quite small and squarish and I was completely baffled about what it might be. I needn't have worried. It was a portable CD player with earphones, and two of my favourite CDs.

"Oh thank you, Mum, thanks Dad. It's brilliant. I know everyone says it, but it really is just what I was wanting, only I never would have dared to ask for such a thing. It must have cost a fortune!"

"You're worth it," said Dad, giving me a hug.

"And now you'll be able to listen to your music without the rest of us also having to listen to it," said Mum, with a cheeky sort of smile.

To fill in the time until Eddy and Laura and their children arrived, we all played a game called Balderdash, which involves making up false definitions to words that nobody's ever heard of. When the doorbell rang, nobody in our family was really in a fit state to answer it, we were all weak with laughing so much.

The next half hour was like a fight to talk because everybody had so much news to catch up on. Tom and Beth were crazy with excitement about their rollerblades, as well as about every other present they'd received. They'd brought most of their presents with them!

"Against our better judgement," said Eddy, rolling his eyes at Mum.

"Did you bring any of your presents with you, Celia?" I asked her, trying to get off to the most friendly start I could.

"Only this," she said, without even looking at me. Her tone of voice was so casual that I thought she was about to show me book or something, but she had gone into the kitchen, then came back with a cage with a hamster in it!

"Oh, isn't he sweet," said Kim, as she and I swooped on the cage to take a better look.

"What's his name?" I asked.

"It's a girl. Brenda," replied Celia.

Kim and I exchanged glances, and then found it almost impossible not to crack up. I mean, Brenda! What a name for a hamster.

"I hope you're not laughing at me," said Celia, turning round suddenly and looking from me to Kim and back again with a very severe expression on her face. "At least Brenda's original, not like Stubbles."

Again Kim and I exchanged glances and I could feel my dislike of Celia coming to the surface.

"Stubbles died last month, actually," said Kim quietly.

Instead of sympathizing, though, Celia said, "Did you replace it?"

"We've got one called Sunny, now," Kim explained in a flat voice. "And we've still got Candlewick." I could tell that she was getting as cross as I felt.

"I thought Sunny belonged to that fat music teacher?" Celia said, as she opened the door to the cage and pulled the sleeping Brenda out of her white woolly cocoon and began playing with her.

"Miss Farrant has died, too," said Kim, probably knowing that I would be unable to speak by now, because I always felt choked when my dear old music teacher's name was mentioned.

"What did she die of?"

"Cancer. Can I hold Brenda for a minute?" Kim changed the subject without even bothering to be subtle. Celia handed the hamster over and walked off towards the kitchen, saying in a whining voice that she was hungry. "Don't let her get to you," Kim whispered as soon as Celia was out of earshot. "She's just insensitive."

"I think I'll go and get Candlewick and Sunny and bring them in for a bit," I said.

"Good idea. I'll help you," Kim offered, putting the hamster back in its cage. "I can't stand red-eyed hamsters anyway," she added, quite agressively for Kim. I had the feeling that had poor Brenda been blessed with brown eyes, Kim would have developed an instant dislike for brown-eyed hamsters.

Lunchtime was good because the adults were drinking wine and cracking jokes the whole time. Kim and I drank wine too, but to be honest I didn't really enjoy mine. It tasted too bitter. The food was wonderful and I ate so much I didn't know how I was ever going to raise the energy to do the treasure hunt.

For some unknown reason Celia started being really nice to everyone at about lunchtime. She seemed to be trying especially hard with me. I thought perhaps she was feeling sorry about Miss Farrant and Stubbles. Whatever the reason, it made the day a whole lot more enjoyable. Mum served the pudding and I felt myself tensing up, wondering whether once again Celia would get the pound coin.

"Are there any coins in it, Auntie Pat?" asked Beth, eyes shining.

"Coins? I don't know what you're talking about," Mum joked. "You don't find coins in puddings, do you?"

"That means there *are*, Beth," Celia informed her sister.

"Don't put anything in your mouth without examining it first," Laura warned Tom and Beth. "And chew for a long time, all right?"

So, there we were, all eating our pudding in thoughtful silence, chewing slowly and thoroughly before swallowing. Eddy came across one of the pound coins and Kim the other, which made everyone clap. Even Celia joined in the clapping and looked happy enough. I had to admit I was surprised, because I hadn't really thought her good mood would survive the ordeal of not getting the piece of pudding with the pound in it. It just showed how wrong I could be. Perhaps Celia was really quite nice and I'd been unfair about her in the past.

"Leah and her friends are going on a trip to Derbyshire," said Mum brightly over coffee and chocolates.

"Lucky girl. When is that, Leah?" Laura asked me.

"The day after tomorrow. I can't wait," I told her happily.

"Are you staying with friends?" asked Eddy.

So the tale of Luce and the competition slowly unfolded and when it was finished, Celia whispered something to her mother. The whisper was loud enough for everyone to hear what she'd said, though.

"Can I go too, Mum?"

Oh no! I thought with horror. OK, Celia was obviously not as bad as I'd thought, but the very last thing I wanted was for her to come along on our special Cafe Club trip. Surely Laura would nip the idea in the bud. I know Mum would have done if I'd said something like that. "You can't just invite yourself along to other people's holidays," Laura said, to my relief.

"But Beth and Tom are staying at Granny and Grandpa Priestly's, and all I'm doing is having a day with them."

"That was your choice, love," said Laura, sounding less sure of herself. I did not like the way this conversation was still going on when it should have stopped ages ago.

"But it's boring at Granny and Grandpa's. You said you understood that I didn't really want to stay for the whole five days, because they always do things for six- and seven-year-olds and not for me."

"Well, it's very difficult for Granny and Grandpa to find things to do that would be suitable for you *and* Beth and Tom," Laura went on. Her voice was sounding almost pleading by now, and I wished Eddy would cut in and tell his wife to drop the subject.

"It's a shame that Celia feels left out," Mum said, tipping her head on one side.

Shut up, Mum, I prayed silently. Don't say any more.

"If I went with Leah and her friends, you and Dad could have some peace with all of us away, couldn't you?" Celia persisted. I saw Laura and Eddy glance at each other and I could just tell that they liked the sound of a bit of peace.

"It's only a very small guest house, though, isn't it?" said Kim, flashing her eyes at Mum. Good old Kim – she was desperately trying to help me out here.

I didn't know if it was the wine, but Mum obviously didn't get the message. In fact, she seemed to be doing her level best to make sure that Celia came on holiday with us, come what may.

"One more little person wouldn't make any difference, I wouldn't have thought," she plunged on. By this time, I was feeling very depressed indeed, but then Dad joined in, which raised my spirits slightly.

"I think it would be best to have a word with Lucy's mother first," he said quietly. "No point in raising hopes only to have them dashed again, is there?"

At last Mum clicked. At least, I think she did. "You're probably right," she said to Dad. I could have hugged him. Then, with Mum's next words, my spirits took a nosedive. "I'll phone her up right now. I expect you'll be wanting to say Happy Christmas to Lucy, won't you, Leah? You usually phone up all your friends on Christmas Day."

"Yes, I was going to phone them to thank them for my presents. I'm surprised Andy hasn't phoned me yet."

The moment I said that, I suddenly realized something. I hadn't had a present from Andy. I'd had something from all of the others, but not from Andy. Kim's mind must have been working along the same lines.

"What did Andy give you for Christmas, Lee?"

"I was just thinking about that. I haven't had a present from Andy, have I?" I was puzzled. I just couldn't work it out.

"Didn't Andy leave a present for Lee with you, Dad, when you played chess with her the other day?"

"What?" Dad frowned in his familiar, scatterbrained way. "Yes, yes she did. I put it under the blanket with all the other presents. I must admit it was very tiny indeed. It's probably still under the window seat, stuck in a corner."

Kim sprang up from her chair and knelt down on the floor to peer under the window seat. She even ran her fingers along the edge of the carpet. "It's not here. That's funny. I hope it hasn't got chucked away with the wrapping paper," she said with a frown. "Just how little was it exactly, Dad?"

"Tiny. Scarcely more than a square centimetre."

"Come on. Wrapping-paper hunt," Kim announced, going off to the kitchen to get the bin.

For the next five minutes all the children thoroughly searched through every scrap of paper, but without success.

"Do you know what the present was, Dad?" I asked him.

"Haven't a clue," he replied.

"And you definitely, definitely put it under the blanket with the other presents?" Kim double-checked.

"Definitely, definitely," Dad assured her, without a trace of uncertainty.

"Well, it must be somewhere," said Mum, and the adults

started searching the whole room. At this point I noticed the expression on Celia's face, and I immediately felt suspicious, because she was looking worried and her eyes kept darting from side to side. I glanced at Kim, who gave me a look that said that she, too, felt suspicious, then she gave me the tiniest jerk of her head as if to say, "Let's go upstairs and discuss this."

A few moments later we'd both managed to sneak away and were talking in whispers on the landing.

"Do you think she's taken it?" asked Kim.

"She looks guilty enough," I replied. "And that would explain why she's being so nice all of a sudden."

"The trouble is, we've got absolutely no way of proving anything."

"Where do you think she's hidden it?"

"It must be in her pocket."

"I don't think she's got any pockets."

We both concentrated hard for a moment, then had the same idea at the same time.

"The hamster's cage," I said.

"You could be right," said Kim. "Let's go and investigate."

We went downstairs and I suggested to my cousins that we look in the kitchen in case the present had dropped out of some wrapping paper. The three of them started to follow me out, but Celia hung back when she saw that Kim wasn't following.

"Coming Kim?" she asked.

"Yeah, you go on, I'll be there in a sec," replied Kim casually.

"I'll just check over here, I think," Celia said. "It doesn't need more than three in the kitchen."

The hamster's cage was by the television in the sitting room, and it was beginning to look as though Celia didn't want to leave it unguarded.

"Oh, look at your poor hamster, Celia," I said, trying a completely different tack.

"What? She's OK. She's asleep."

I think she's wilting from the heat of the fire. I'll move her over here."

"It's OK, I'll move her," Celia said in a loud voice as she leapt across the room and picked up the cage. Kim and I exchanged looks. "I thought you were going to phone Lucy," added Celia in a firm voice.

"Yes, I was, wasn't I?" I took the phone up to my room and tapped in Andy's number.

"Hi."

"Hi, Andy. Happy Christmas."

"Hi, Lee. You've beaten me by about three seconds. I even had the receiver in my hand! Thanks for the speedometer. It's brilliant. I've already tried it out."

"That's OK. Andy, we can't find your present to me. Dad said he put it under the blanket with the other parcels, but it's simply vanished."

"It was very teeny."

"The thing is, Kim and I think that our cousin Celia might have taken it. We may be wrong, but she's acting guilty. I was just phoning to ask you what the present is, because it'll be easier if we know what we're looking for."

"It's an anklet."

"An anklet! Oh, that's a lovely present, Andy. I really hope it turns up. I'd love to have an anklet. Kim and I have a feeling that it may be in Celia's hamster's cage, but Celia is making sure we don't get near it. Is it just a plain chain?"

"No, it's got little tiny keys hanging all along it. They're absolutely minute."

"The other bad thing that's happened is that Celia is trying to get herself invited to come away with us."

"Oh dear," replied Andy. If it had been Luce she would have started jibbering and squealing and protesting, but not Andy. That's not her way of carrying on. "Give me a ring later, and tell me if you've found the anklet, and whether or not Celia has managed to get her way."

"Yeah, OK."

"Good luck."

We rang off and I went downstairs to find that the search had been called off and everyone was choosing teams for charades.

"What did Lucy say?" Celia asked me immediately.

"I phoned Andy instead. She said her present was an anklet. She's really upset that it's disappeared into thin air." I was watching the expression on Celia's face when I said this, but she didn't bat an eyelid. She just looked sympathetic and said that she didn't mind carrying on searching if I wanted to.

"Oh Celia, that's really kind of you," said Mum, "but the whole day's going to go by without any games being played if we're not careful."

"And then there's Dad's treasure hunt, isn't there?" Kim reminded us all.

"There certainly is," said Dad.

"Let's do it straight away," Kim said. "Wouldn't you rather do a treasure hunt than play charades?" she asked Beth and Tom.

"What's the treasure?" Tom wanted to know.

"Ah! It's a secret," teased Dad.

"I want to do the treasure hunt straight away!" said Beth, jumping up and down, then jumping round and round in a circle.

"Right, treasure hunt it is," said Dad. "Everybody'll have to go out for a walk or something while I put the clues out."

"I know, why don't I help you with the clues, Dad?" Kim said, and I held my breath, because this would be the perfect opportunity to search the hamster's cage while Celia was out of the house.

"No, no, no," said Dad. "I'm the only person who's allowed to know the clues. Everybody out! Come on, move along there!"

So we were all ushered out, and given strict instructions to stay out for at least twenty minutes. In the end it was exactly nineteen minutes before we went back in, because Beth was so excited about the treasure hunt that she couldn't last out a moment longer.

Kim and I had gone striding on ahead of the others so that we could have a private discussion. We'd decided to wait until Celia was out of the sitting room, then I would pretend to be looking for a clue in the hamster cage. But as it happened, there was no need for me to do that. . .

Chapter 3

Andy

"Take care," Mum said as we stood on the platform. She had cupped my face in her hands, which she often did when she was saying goodbye to me. Her hands felt very soft and cool, and her eyes looked right into mine. "Don't do anything dangerous, will you?"

"No, don't worry, Mum."

"I *do* worry. I can't help it with a daughter like you, *bibiche*."

Mum's hands dropped to her side and she gave me a kiss. She smelt of expensive perfume. It was her usual sort and I loved the smell of it. It was the one thing that would stay in my mind when I got on the train. Even when I couldn't smell it any more I would still be able to bring it to mind. Dad didn't come to see me off because he was in France, so Mum would feel quite at a loss with half her family missing.

Further down the platform Luce was saying a very dramatic farewell to her twin brothers whose guts she hates most of the time. Jaimini was saying goodbye to her parents and Leah was hugging her sister, Kim, which got me thinking, Thank goodness we're not saddled with the company of cousin Celia. It was a pretty close shave, though. Fen and Tash were already on the train with Helen and Peta, so I gave Mum one more kiss, repeated that there was nothing to worry about and got on the train, followed by Luce, Leah and Jaimini.

As the train pulled away, all the others waved their parents right out of sight, but I didn't because I always have the feeling that if I wave anyone I care about out of sight, I'll be waving them out of my life. Mum knows this about me, so she blew me a kiss and went. I know it's only a stupid superstition, but I stick to my gut feeling on this one.

"Right, tell us exactly what happened on the Cousin Celia front," said Luce, leaning forwards, eyes shining, once everyone was installed in their seats with the long journey ahead. Helen was sitting in the corner with Peta next to her. Normally the presence of an adult would cramp our style slightly, but with Helen it matters less than with any of the others. She's very laid-back, even though she's very protective of her family. She somehow manages to do it in a less obvious way than most, yet you'd expect it to be the reverse because of her being a single parent.

Peta was on her best behaviour and we were all pretty surprised about that because normally she would at the very least be showing off in front of us six, and on an exciting journey like this, she'd be right over the top. But so far, so good. Helen must have given her some kind of warning. Whatever it was, it was working.

"Come on, Andy, we're dying to hear what happened," persisted Luce.

"There's nothing to tell, really. I put down the phone from talking to Leah and suddenly registered that she'd said something about a hamster that Celia had brought with her, and I thought maybe, just maybe. . . I mean, that would be the obvious place, wouldn't it, so rather than phone back, I asked Mum if I could go for a walk."

"If I asked *my* mum if I could go for a walk on Christmas Day she'd either think I was out of my tree or otherwise she'd suspect that I was up to no good," Luce said, looking round at the others for agreement on this point.

"My mummy would fink I'd fallen on the carpet," Peta informed us, big-eyed.

Helen smiled to herself and got Peta back to her colouring. The rest of us all laughed except Luce, who knitted her eyebrows together.

"Peta reckons that falling on the carpet is something like being 'out of your tree'," explained Jaimini patiently.

"Oh, I get it," said Luce, grinning round at the rest of us, which made us laugh even more.

"You take over from here Lee. I've lost the thread," I said.

"I'm good at finding fings," piped up Peta. "Where d'you drop your fred, Andy?"

I could tell this journey was going to be an entertaining one, with Peta around. "I've not lost anything really," I said, as the others smothered their giggles.

"Come on, Lee, we're all desperate to hear the end of this Celia thing," Fen said, so Leah took over.

"Right, well, we went for our walk so that Dad could put out the clues for the treasure hunts and when we got back, Dad was playing draughts with Andy. I couldn't believe my eyes!"

"Why, because they normally play chess?" asked Luce.

"No, because Andy was there in the first place," Leah explained.

Fen and I were the only two to find that funny. It often

happens like that. In many ways Fen and I are on the same wavelength.

"No more interruptions, Luce. We're going to be there in two hours and I would quite like to hear this story before then," said Jaimini, which made everybody lean slightly towards Leah so that she could continue uninterrupted.

"Anyway, as we all trooped into the house, everybody said hi to Andy, then Andy said to Celia, 'I was just admiring your hamster. Did you get it for Christmas?' and Celia immediately looked worried and said, 'Yes, she's called Brenda, only I don't want to keep getting her out because they sleep during the day, and apparently when they first go to new owners it's really important that they don't disturb their routine, because it's a big enough readjustment for them to have new people to get used to and they don't take to the smell of some people, you know.'"

"Is that true – that they've got to keep to their routine and all that?" asked Fen.

"I've heard the bit about the smell before," said Jaimini. "I think that bit may be true."

"I've no idea," said Leah. "All I knew was that she was rambling on frantically, which made her seem even more guilty in my eyes. Anyway, Andy calmly said, 'Oh, don't worry, I won't disturb her again, although she didn't wake up when I reached into her cage and gave her a stroke.' Well, you should have seen the look on Celia's face then. She went very pale and big-eyed, and Andy carried on in exactly the same tone of voice to say, 'By the way, I found this in her cage,' and she held out my anklet in the palm of her hand.

"There was dead silence in the room at that moment because nobody knew what to say. It was my dad who filled the silence by saying to Andy, 'Now, where were we? My move I think.' And the two of them carried on with their game of draughts as though there hadn't been any interruption at all."

"What happened next?" asked Tash in a shaky voice. Poor Tash hates it when people don't get on with each other, or when there's any sort of clash.

"Well, Celia's dad, Uncle Eddy, said that he wanted a word with Celia and he took her outside into the garden, while Mum said she was going to put the kettle on and she and Laura went through to the kitchen. Kim put on some album or other that she'd got for Christmas and began to dance with Tom and Beth, who hadn't really realized that anything was wrong, and I sat down with Andy and Dad and followed the rest of their game, while Andy apologized about a million times for making Celia look such a fool in public, and Dad assured her about a million times that she'd done it brilliantly, and that it had to be done in front of everyone to make the point properly. Dad said that he thought Celia would never do anything like that again.

"When she and Uncle Eddy came back from the garden, Celia looked a bit tearful, but everybody pretended that they hadn't really noticed and actually Celia then made a big effort to be nice for the rest of the day and we all had great fun together. She even apologized to me and said she didn't know what made her do it. I didn't really know what to say, but I felt sorry for her."

"Was she banned from coming on holiday with us because of all that?" asked Fen.

"Nothing more was said on the subject, but I presume that's what did it," Leah replied.

"Can I have a hamster, Mummy?" asked Peta a few seconds later.

"One day," replied Helen, a little absent-mindedly.

"Monday?" asked Peta.

"No."

"Toosday?"

"No."

"What's next, Tasha?"

"Wednesday."

"Not Wednesday, Thursday, Friday, Saturday or Sunday," said Helen, obviously trying to bring this conversation to an end. "One day when you're older."

"When I'm four?"

Helen looked up from her book with an exasperated look, then she saw Peta's earnest little face looking quizzically up at her, and said, "Yes, I expect so."

Then Peta poked her head through the gap betwen her seat and Helen's, so that she was looking at the people in the seats behind us, and said, "I'm having a hamster when I'm four."

"Oh, that's nice." "Lovely." "Aren't you a lucky girl," said our enthusiastic fellow-travellers. Peta withdrew her head like a tortoise going back into its shell, then poked it back again and added, "Called Bumper," which brought on some more hearty replies from the people behind and a load of stifled giggles from us.

"Why don't you draw Bumper in his cage?" suggested Helen, and for the next ten minutes there was silence from Peta, apart from her noises of concentration, which were like breathy little coughs.

Tash

The train journey must have seemed very long to Peta, and maybe even longer to Mum, who had to keep Peta entertained. We tried having her sit with us and play I-spy, but that didn't work because she was far too young to understand how to play, so we played at spotting things out of the train window instead, but she got bored with that after about a minute. Next we tried a game of shutting our eyes and then opening them and guessing which of the six of us was holding the ten-pence piece in our hands. This went down very well indeed, only this time it was us who got bored. Peta would happily have played "find the ten-pence piece" till the end of the journey, but Mum rescued us and took Peta off for a walk down the train in search of sandwiches.

Jules and her mum, Luce's Auntie Alice, met us at the station in two cars. I went with Fen, Leah and Andy in Jules's car, and the others went with Auntie Alice. Jules seemed really nice. She chatted like mad. The only thing that was slightly worrying was that she kept turning towards Fen, who was sitting in the front, to talk to her, and that meant she took her eyes off the road. Once she even turned right round to look at Andy, and I was sure she was going to crash into something. In the end we asked Jules if she could slow down a bit so we could admire the countryside. It really was true that we wanted to take in absolutely everything because it was all so different from where we live. We couldn't believe how wild and rugged it looked and how rolling and wonderful the hills were, with dry-stone walls dividing all the fields and turning the landscape into a patchwork quilt. At times it took my breath away. When the journey was over we all piled out with our luggage and I began to feel even more excited.

Auntie Alice led the way inside, turning round so often that it probably would have been easier for her to walk backwards. I found myself wondering if this turning round thing was something that ran in the family! The other thing that Jules and Auntie Alice had in common was a love of tea. They both mentioned having a nice pot of tea about ten times. But there the family resemblance ended because Auntie Alice was plump with fair skin and freckles, and hair that was fair mixed with grey. She also had grey eyes and big cheeks, whereas Jules was about the same height but slim with dark hair, darker skin and brown eyes. I decided that Jules must take after her dad, and I started to wonder whether we would meet him. Luce hadn't said anything about an uncle, so I didn't even know if he was around.

Both Jules and Auntie Alice were very friendly and wanted to know all about us. Their Derbyshire accents were lovely to listen to and we all liked the way they called us things like "love" and "dear" and even "duck" at the end of every single sentence. We were told to choose whichever rooms we wanted then to come and have a nice pot of tea. This was the best bit. I love looking at bedrooms. We let Mum choose which room she wanted for herself and Peta first, and she chose quite a small room but the view was lovely. She also had an ensuite bathroom. Of the other three rooms, only one had an ensuite bathroom but this was the one with the worst view. Luce was desperate for this room and Jaimini said she didn't mind, so that became their room. Fen and I tossed a coin with Leah and Andy for the biggest bedroom and Leah and Andy won. I was glad, because I would have felt too sorry for them if they'd lost to enjoy being in that room myself. Leah suggested that we swap over halfway through the week, but Fen and I said we really didn't mind at all, and then we discovered that the room that we were having was the only one with a proper full-length mirror in it, so everything seemed equal then.

Fen wanted the bed nearest the window and I wanted the one nearest the door, so that worked out well, too. We quickly unpacked, which didn't take any time at all because we'd all travelled with the bare minimum. In fact we'd got together and drawn up a list of what to take so we all had more or less the same clothes, except that one or two of us had substituted a long skirt for a pair of smarter trousers. As far as make-up and jewellery is concerned, we're all completely different. Andy only wears a ring, which Jacques gave her (Jacques is her French sort-of boyfriend). Jaimini and Luce both have pierced ears and I know Luce packed loads of different earrings, all big and dangly, whereas Jaimini only usually wears studs with different-coloured stones in them.

Leah and I like wearing necklaces and we all wear friendship bracelets, and Fen has phases on jewellery and times when she's right off it. Luce wears the most make-up out of us all, followed by me, then Fen, then Jaimini, then Leah, then Andy, who never wears make-up at all.

Once we were all downstairs and sitting in the dining room – just like proper guests having their afternoon tea – we got even more excited and couldn't stop talking about our rooms and discussing what time we'd all have breakfast, who was going to have a shower and who was going to have a bath, who wanted to explore the town and things like that. Jules had made a lovely log fire and we sat round it with our muffins and hot chocolate, feeling cosy and contented.

Auntie Alice just kept smiling at all of us and telling Luce how lucky she was to have such a lovely bunch of friends. Jules wanted to know all about our Cafe Club, and said she'd have to tell the local cafe owner that there were six experienced girls in town if he was short-staffed.

"Does anyone mind if I go out for a walk?" Andy asked. I was surprised that she'd managed to last out as long as she had, because Andy gets restless so easily, and after that long train journey *and* sitting down drinking tea she must have been desperate to get moving.

"How about you lot all going out and having a look round the town? I'll take Peta out and we'll go at a slower pace, then we'll meet up again in a couple of hours and take it from there," Helen suggested.

"Great," Fen replied for us all.

"And girls," said Mum, as we all scraped our chairs back to stand up, "let's just get a couple of ground rules established shall we, then we'll all know where we are?" I glanced at the others, feeling slightly anxious in case they thought Mum was getting heavy, but they were looking completely normal. "Don't go off anywhere without telling someone where you're going. If I give you a time to be back, make sure you always come back at that time and not a minute later, otherwise I won't let you go off the next time you want to. If you split up with each other make sure you make proper arrangements for meeting up again, and always keep the telephone number and address of this guest house either written down or in your head. I know that must sound as though I'm being very restrictive, but I'm just thinking of your safety, and within those rules you've got a lot of freedom. Is everybody happy with all that?"

Again I glanced at the others to check that they didn't

feel like they were at school, but they were all nodding vigorously and assuring Mum that they didn't think that was over the top, and that of course they'd always make sure that they were back on time. We then all learnt the phone number and the address by heart.

'OK, synchronize watches," said Luce, sticking her wrist out. We all did the same and nobody had to change their watch because they all said the same time – three twenty-one. "Back here at five twenty-one," Luce told the rest of us as though she was in charge. I saw Mum smile at Auntie Alice.

"I think five thirty will be fine."

And off we went.

Jaimini

We were about five minutes away from the guest house, which, incidentally, was called West Lea Guest House and was on a road called West Road, when I suddenly realized that we hadn't set eyes on the dog that Jules was supposed to be house-sitting for. When I mentioned this to the others, Luce said she'd like to go back for it and take it on our walk with us, but the rest of us weren't so keen, so instead we contented ourselves with guessing what sort of dog we all thought it was going to turn out to be and what its name was. Personally I guessed it was a golden labrador called Tirallee. Goodness knows where that name came from. It just popped into my head. Luce guessed it would be a sausage dog called Bernard, and I can't remember what the others thought.

We found the local cafe in no time at all, right in the middle of the High Street. Luce and I were quite keen to go in and have a look and so were Tash and Leah, but Fen said she'd go mad if she had to look at another cup of tea, and Andy said she didn't want to sit down, she wanted to walk, so those two went off together and we went into the cafe. After less than a minute Fen and Andy came back and we all thought they'd changed their minds, but they hadn't, they'd just remembered what Helen had said about always making sure that we made proper arrangements for meeting up again. It made us all realize how sensible Helen's rules were, because we would have worried about where Fen and Andy had got to if we'd got back to the guest house to find that they hadn't yet arrived. We agreed to meet at this sort of statue thing that we could see in the distance, in forty minutes.

It felt funny sitting together in a cafe that was more or less the same size as "our" cafe, but not knowing the people who ran it at all. There was a girl of about sixteen waitressing, along with two women of roughly the same age as Jan.

"I bet their chef isn't as good-looking as Kevin," said Luce, looking round as though she expected the chef suddenly to appear and confirm her suspicions.

"I bet he's not even as *good* as Kevin," said Tash.

At that point one of the older waitresses came to take our order.

"Chocolate milkshake for me, please," said Luce.

"Me too," I said, and the other two decided to have the same.

"Not from round here, are you?" said the waitress, smiling. I wasn't sure whether she thought it was our accents or our faces that didn't fit. We must have looked upset because she immediately put her hand on my shoulder and said in a very apologetic, embarrassed voice, "Just listen to me! It's really none of my business where you come from or who you are, for that matter. It's just that I've never seen you in here before."

We explained that we were from Cableden and told her we were staying at West Lea Guest House. We were careful not to say that the owners were away, because we didn't want to invite burglars in.

"Well, I hope you have a lovely week my dears. You wouldn't catch me staying in that guest house for all the tea in China, I may tell you, but then I've never been very good with things that go bump in the night and I couldn't stomach that dog at any price!" Well *that* time the alarm must have really shown on our faces because again she put her hand on my shoulder. "Oh there I go again, saying the first thing that comes into my head. Just ignore me, eh?" She smiled round at us all, but we didn't feel like ignoring her after that dramatic statement.

"Is the place haunted or something?" asked Luce.

"Well, nobody really knows, but there's nothing to worry about. There's a lovely friendly atmosphere by all accounts."

"What's wrong with the dog?" I asked, but I never did get a reply because the waitress had rushed off. We could see her telling the young waitress to get our drinks. She was smiling and pointing to our table but the young waitress was scowling. Goodness knew why.

"Ouch! I can't stop scratching!" Luce suddenly said as she tried to scratch her left hip through her trousers.

"It's the middle of winter, Luce," I reminded her. "I don't think there are many insects on the prowl." Then she began to attack the other hip with the same vigour.

"That's a bit of a coincidence, isn't it?" Tash said. "You're scratching in exactly the same place on both hips."

"Perhaps it's an insect that likes things to be symmetrical," giggled Leah. "Sorry Luce," she quickly added, seeing that Luce wore a very unimpressed look.

"I know what it is! It's these new jeans," said Luce. "I get that sometimes with jeans. The studs make me itch."

"What, like an allergy?" I asked.

"I don't know, but it happened with my last jeans. I need to get some antihistamine cream, then I'll be all right."

At that point the young waitress appeared with our drinks. She looked very sulky indeed and plonked the drinks down so that every single one of them spilled. I couldn't work out what her problem was, and neither could the others. I saw Leah smile nervously at her, which was typical of Leah, trying to be kind even when someone was being horrible.

"You a model or something?" the girl asked Leah.

"No. I—"

"Because you needn't come lording it in here."

"I—"

Suddenly I realized that this girl had obviously got a big chip on her shoulder about something, and she was taking it out on Leah just because Leah had smiled at her. She must have misinterpreted the smile as a sort of smug sneer, as though Leah's smile was meaning, "Poor you, with your frizzy permed hair and your pasty face. But I'm all right with my beautiful looks, so I can afford to smile at you."

But Leah had gone pink and was biting her bottom lip and suddenly I snapped. I don't usually snap, but this girl was way out of line and I just had to defend Leah.

"Look, we're just sitting here minding our own business. What's *with* you?"

I heard Luce's sharp intake of breath and it crossed my mind very fleetingly that this was a complete role reversal for Luce and me, because it's usually her saying the outrageous things and me with the sharp intake of breath. I saw the girl's lips tighten. There was just one milkshake left for her to plonk down and it was Leah's. The others had sloshed, but this one she looked as though she was going to put down carefully on the table, for some unknown reason. I watched her, because I couldn't believe that Leah was going to get away with not a drop spilled. The next bit seemed to happen in slow motion.

"Don't yer talk posh?" the girl said, turning to me with a look of mock sympathy. This meant that she wasn't looking where she was putting the milkshake.

"Watch out!" Luce squeaked and I saw that the milkshake was balancing on the very edge of the table. Leah immediately made a grab for it, but she was too late and most of the contents of the glass slid into a chocolate pool in her lap, and then slid down her jeans.

"Omigod!" squeaked Leah as she jumped up.

"Well," that were a clumsy thing to do," the girl said, giving Leah a hard look.

"She didn't do anything," Luce and Tash both said at the same time.

"You didn't put it down properly," I said, matching the girl's hard stare.

"Course I did. She just knocked it over with 'er 'and."

"Can you get me a cloth or something?" Leah asked in a small voice. "I'm soaked!" I noticed that the older waitress was rushing over with three cloths and a towel, looking very brisk and mother hen-ish.

"What did your last servant die of, Little Miss Posh?" said the girl as her parting shot. She'd deliberately said it under her breath to make sure that the approaching waitress couldn't hear her. I heard, though, and it made me mad. Leah looked as though she was about to burst into tears and Tash and Luce both looked very uncomfortable.

"Dearie me, let's get you sorted out," the kind older waitress said as she handed Leah a cloth and fussed around her, wiping the table and the floor. "I'll get Emma to bring you another drink, dear. Accidents will happen, even to the best of us, eh?" She was patting Leah's shoulder as if to reassure her that it didn't matter.

Emma was clearing a nearby table but watching and listening to what was going on at ours at the same time. Her eyes met mine and a look of triumph came over her face. Her eyes seemed to be saying, "Looks like I got away with that one, doesn't it?" I'd been on the point of dobbing on her the moment the older waitress had arrived with the cloths, but then I'd changed my mind because it seemed like school all of a sudden, so I'd decided not to say anything. But when Emma gave me that supercilious look I just *had* to defend poor Leah, especially as the older waitress obviously thought that it was Leah who had tipped over the milkshake.

"It wasn't Leah's fault," I said in an indignant whisper, so as not to attract any more attention. "That waitress wasn't looking what she was doing and she put the milkshake down on the very edge of the table."

"Oh, it was Emma, was it?" asked the waitress, her smiling face clouding over rather abruptly. I looked over to where Emma was now making coffee just in time to see her look daggers at Leah. She'd obviously heard me dobbing on her, but I think she thought it had been Leah who had spoken. Either way, she was *not* happy.

We didn't stay long after that, because we felt uncomfortable with Emma casting nasty glances in our direction all the time. Leah and I went into the loos and she stood on a chair with the hand-dryer going full blast on her jeans. They took about five minutes to dry, and even then weren't done completely, but they were certainly much better. Then we beat a hasty retreat and went to buy some antihistamine for Luce, before meeting up with Andy and Fen.

Chapter 4

Fen

Andy was in the mood for quick walking. We walked right to the other side of the town. Then we carried on walking, even though we seemed to have left the town behind. The cars were thinning out, and there was a park on one side of the road and a few houses on the other. We went into the park.

"You didn't want to look at shops or anything, did you?" asked Andy.

"It's a bit late to ask me that, isn't it?"

She glanced at my face quickly to check I wasn't seriously hacked off about not shopping. I wasn't. We were heading towards the swings, but Andy suddenly stopped and picked something up.

"What is it?" I asked, as we both examined the S-shaped piece of silver metal. Andy didn't answer, but put it in her pocket. "What do you want to keep it for?"

"Souvenir."

Andy never says all that much, and sometimes it's really hard to know how her mind is working. This was one of those times. We both had a go on the swings, then the see-saw.

"Aren't we babies?" I giggled as we went up and down.

"Let's have a go on there, shall we?" Andy said. She nodded towards the main part of the play area, which was a brilliant mixture of apparatus to climb and swing on, walk along, jump over and slide down. It was designed for little kids, but it *did* look like really good fun. There was a sort of house that you could reach from three different sides. It was just a small enclosed area, but it had a roof on it and something that looked like a chimney. You could either climb a rope or a steep ramp to get to it or go along a bridge that moved as you walked. Once you were in the house, you could slide down the slide to get back to ground level.

I went back to the swing and watched Andy make her way up to the bridge, which she nimbly ran across to get into the house. As I gently swung myself back and forth I felt sure I could hear Andy talking, so I stopped to listen. I was right. It was impossible to hear if there were two voices or just Andy's, and I wondered if she was singing to herself.

"Andy," I called. She didn't answer and my curiosity got the better of me. I went up the ramp and bent right down to get into the little house. It was gloomy inside. Andy was sitting cross-legged opposite another girl of about our age, who was also cross-legged.

"This is Fen," said Andy, without looking at me.

"Hi," said the girl. She was thin, with chin-length mousey hair. She was wearing black faded jeans and a big woolly jacket. She didn't smile at me. The only thought that was going through my mind was how on earth Andy had managed to strike up a conversation so quickly with this girl. It wasn't like Andy to get into conversation with anyone, but definitely not with a pretty unfriendly-looking stranger who was sitting in a kids' play house. Or perhaps that was it. Maybe they hit it off immediately because they were two thirteen-year-olds in a kids' play area.

"It's this kind of club I'm in. Well, it's more of an organization really," the girl said to Andy.

"The S dropped out of my pocket," Andy explained to me. "It belongs to—"

"Sid," the girl said. "I can't believe I lost it," she went on, with an irritated frown as though she was cross with herself.

"Well, never mind, at least you've got it back now," Andy said in a matter-of-fact voice. The girl levelled her gaze at Andy and the two of them studied each other as hard as they could. That's the thing about Andy. She doesn't communicate like the rest of us do. There aren't many people like her, but I reckoned that this girl was one person who would get on well with her.

"We've got a club too," I said politely. "It's called the Cafe Club."

"Uh-huh," replied the girl. I decided to shut up.

"I'm Andy," said Andy.

Suddenly Andy and Sid grinned at each other. I thought I must have missed something, but then I caught on. Andy and Sid are both boys' names. The two girls were just registering that they had something in common. Most girls of our age would make some sort of remark about what a coincidence it was, but not Andy, and apparently not Sid, either.

"What do you do in your organization?" asked Andy. I had been wanting to ask that, but I thought it might sound a bit of an obvious question. I was glad that Andy had asked it.

"I can't really tell you that."

"Why not?" I asked.

"Is it to do with this?" asked Andy, holding up the S.

Sid ignored me and nodded at Andy.

"Do you all wear one of these?" Andy asked next.

"Uh-huh."

There was a short silence before Sid's next words.

"You're not from round here, are you?"

"We're on holiday," I told her.

"For how long?"

"A week."

"When d'you get here?"

"Today."

"Hm. What made you come to the park?"

"We didn't feel like shopping," I replied.

For the first time she looked properly at me. "What d'you say your name was?"

"Fen."

"Funny name."

I could have said, "Well, it's short for Fenella, actually," but I decided not to. I somehow didn't think that Sid would like the name Fenella.

"Our friends are in the cafe," Andy said.

"How many of them?"

"Four."

"Uh-huh." She turned to me again. "Actually, it's a nice name, Fen." She smiled and her face changed completely. My eyes had adjusted to the dim light and I thought she looked quite pretty.

"We'd better be going," I said to Andy.

"Yeah, you're right," Andy replied, wriggling onto the top of the slide. She slid down and I followed her, wondering if Sid would do the same, but she didn't.

"See you, Sid," I called, as Andy and I started to walk away.

Her head appeared out of another hole and she spoke to Andy. "If you're interested in joining, we're called the Strays. It's not easy to join, though. You have to be the right kind of person and you have to pass a kind of test."

"Go on," said Andy, leaning forward and looking interested.

"You need to find an S, like this one – I mean, one each."

"Where are we supposed to look?" I asked.

"There are quite a few of them hidden in Bracken Valley. It's a brilliant place to explore, but even more brilliant if you've got an aim. The Strays spent ages hiding the Ss there. If and when you find one, you just let me know."

"Where will we find you?"

"If you come here, one of *us* will find *you*. I'll tell the others about you. But don't go blabbing about us." Andy frowned when Sid said that. "Sorry, I know you won't. It's just what we always have to say. You know. I wouldn't even have said this much if you lived round here."

It all sounded very mysterious, but also quite exciting. I bet Andy would have liked to have clicked her fingers and found herself in the middle of Bracken Valley right there and then. Her eyes were shining like they always do when she's about to embark on an adventure.

"OK," she said simply to Sid, then we both turned again and set off at a jog, because we'd be late back at the meeting place otherwise. As we jogged we talked.

"Did you like her?" I asked Andy.

"Yeah."

"I wonder what the Strays actually do," I said. Andy looked thoughtful.

"I don't know but I'd love to find out. Wouldn't you?"

"I'd certainly love to go S-hunting in Bracken Valley," I replied. And we both laughed as we made our way back to the centre of the town.

Tash

It wasn't till we were making our way back to the guest house that Jaimini suddenly remembered what the waitress had said to us about "things that go bump in the night" and about not being able to "stomach that dog at any price". That got us thinking about what kind of dog it might be, and also about why we hadn't seen it on our earlier visit.

Mum and Peta were arriving at West Lea at exactly the same moment as us, only from the opposite direction. Peta was holding a lead. On the end of it was the ugliest old dog you've ever seen. I've no idea what breed he was: probably a mongrel. He was dripping saliva and he started to growl when he drew level with us.

"Is he safe, Mum?"

"Nobody likes him 'cept me," Peta told us, as she gave the growly old beast a sharp tap on the nose and said, "Stop that, Twister!" The dog immediately stopped growling. "Sit, Twister!" The dog sat.

"Peta, you ought to be a dog trainer when you grow up," Jaimini told her, which made her launch into a million instructions for the poor confused animal. He'd got short, thick, pinky-brown hair and one eye seemed to be higher than the other. He was a most peculiar shape, and all in all, didn't have a lot going for him.

"Nobody guessed his name right," said Luce.

"The waitress in the café was very rude about him," I told Mum, "which wasn't very nice of her, because he can't help being ugly, can he?"

Jules had left us a note to say that she'd be back later, so we all had sausage, egg and chips, which Mum had bought, followed by apple strudel, also bought by Mum. Then we scoured the local paper and found that there was a really good film showing at the local cinema. Mum said it was fine for us to go, as long as we got a taxi back, so she booked the taxi and we went off to get ready.

It was when I was on my own in mine and Fen's room that I first heard the noises. I don't think I would have taken any notice of them if the waitress hadn't mentioned "things that go bump in the night". It was like the faintest tapping noise and because I was in a strange place, and didn't know what noises were normal, I just thought that it must be the heating, or the water tank filling up. All the same I went to get Mum to listen, but typically, the noise stopped before Mum got there.

When she'd gone back downstairs again, I distinctly heard a few more taps. I rushed over to Andy's room to get Fen and they both came back together to listen for the tapping. Once again, the noise stopped, though. It was almost as though there was a ghost who had it in for *me*, and me only. He or she didn't want to scare anyone else. Goodness knows what I'd done to deserve that.

Leah

Andy was really indignant about what had happened in the cafe. She couldn't believe that anyone could have been so horrible as that Emma girl had been. I told her the whole story as we were walking back to the guest house.

"And you didn't say anything that may have upset her — by mistake, obviously?"

"No, she was scowling from the very first moment that she set eyes on us, as though she simply didn't want us in the cafe. All I did was smile at her, because I thought that would show her that we were nice. Then she seemed to get more and more grumpy, especially with Jaimini when she defended me. But she called her posh, Andy, and gave me horrible looks. Then she finished off by tipping a milkshake all down me."

"Do you think she did it on purpose?"

"I don't know. My mind was on something else at the time, but Jaimini said afterwards that she was sure she'd done it on purpose. The manageress looked pretty cross about it all when Jaimini told her what had happened."

"Jaimini dobbed on the waitress?"

"Well yeah, she was only defending me. The manageress thought I'd knocked it over through my own clumsiness."

"I bet that made the waitress mad."

"Yeah, she looked daggers in our direction. We won't be going back to *that* cafe again in a hurry."

Andy didn't say anything for a moment, but I know her well, and she would have been thinking about it all. It sounded like Jaimini was being a real sneak when I told the story, but anyone who'd been there and seen how horrible Emma was would understand why Jaimini had said something to the manageress.

"What was your mind on at the time?" Andy suddenly said to me.

I didn't think she'd noticed me saying that as I'd slipped it into the conversation so quickly, and the moment the words were out of my mouth, I'd regretted them. You see, I'd noticed the most lovely-looking boy of about my age or a bit older sitting with another boy and two girls at the other side of the cafe. I'd actually spotted him the moment I'd walked in, and I'd had a really difficult job keeping my eyes off him after that. I'm not like Luce, I don't fall in love at the drop of a hat, and I'd no idea what it was about this boy that I liked so much. He wasn't really what you'd call good-looking, there was just something in his eyes and the way he was talking with the others at his table that made me wish I could meet him. That's the only reason why I didn't see the milkshake falling in the first place. I'm not usually that dozy. The big question now was whether I ought to tell Andy the truth about what my mind had been on at the time. It sounded so pathetic, and I didn't want Andy to get the wrong idea.

"I know you'll think I'm stupid, but it was a boy."

Andy didn't say anything at first, which was typical of her. She never rushes into making judgements, and flashing her opinions around.

"Yeah?" she asked, encouraging me to go on.

"There's nothing to tell, really. I saw him at a table with three other people. I thought he looked nice. I wished I could have met him . . . then we went."

"So he didn't notice *you*?"

I felt myself blushing and tried to stop it. "I think he did, actually," I admitted, remembering the wonderful moment when our eyes had met. He'd looked away immediately, but had looked back a moment later and given me a kind of half-smile. Only then I'd looked down, because I didn't want him to think I was flirting.

"A-ha!" said Andy. "So this could explain why the waitress—"

"Emma."

"— Emma, decided to treat you to a pair of wet jeans. Maybe this boy was strictly *her* territory and she caught you looking at him, and then she caught *him* looking at you, and she didn't like it."

Andy's words had shocked me. I'd never connected the milkshake incident with that boy. But now I thought about it, I realized that Andy must be right.

"Did any of the others notice you and the boy?"

"No, at least I don't think so," I said in a rush. "And I don't want to talk about it to anyone else. I'll probably never ever see him again anyway, but I feel stupid now, so please don't say anything to the others."

"You know I won't," Andy assured me. And I did know.

Chapter 5

Andy

The film was a comedy. It was a bit too slapstick for me. I'm not really into that kind of thing. I could hear Leah and Tash on either side of me laughing away, but I was deep in my own thoughts. Thoughts about Sid. I wished I knew more about her. She was different from anyone I'd ever met. I had the feeling that she must have lead a tough life. I also wanted to know more about the Strays: what they did, where they met, that kind of thing. It was obvious there was no way to know any of these things until you actually became a member of the club. It was a challenge that Sid had thrown out to me, finding an S. It was a brilliant idea, because anyone who didn't go for the challenge wouldn't be the right kind of person for the club anyway. The more I thought about it, the more intrigued I felt. I hadn't said anything to Leah about the Strays yet, and as far as I knew, Fen hadn't told anyone. Somehow we'd all been so wrapped up in the story about what had happened at the cafe that we hadn't got round to talking about what Fen and I had been doing. It was Tash who eventually asked us and Fen said we'd been to the park and met this girl called Sid, but she hadn't gone on to say anything about the Strays, so neither had I. It was just as though the time wasn't quite right. Or maybe Fen had sussed that I didn't want to talk about it, so had kept quiet for my sake. I didn't know and it wasn't that important.

In a way I wished I could go outside and start looking for Ss instead of watching this film. But that would have been impossible. For one thing it was pitch black outside. All the same, I thought that if I had to sit still with this unfunny film going on in front of me for a minute longer I'd go mad.

"I'm just going to the loo," I whispered to Leah as I got up to go. I could see people's faces dimly as I walked towards the exit sign. They all wore the same broad smiles. One face, though, made me stop in my tracks. It wasn't the face. It was the S on the chain round the girl's neck. I couldn't even be certain that it *was* an S in the gloom, and I certainly couldn't stand there staring so I kept on walking. All the way to the loo I could see the image of this silver S glinting in the darkness. Or was it an S? There was quite a high chance that it was nothing more than my overactive imagination wanting to see an S, and so conjuring one up. It seemed all too much of a coincidence that I'd come across someone wearing an S so soon after I'd been given the task of finding that very thing. Unless, of course, there were loads and loads of people in the Strays.

By the time I'd got back into the cinema itself I'd decided what to do. I would sit down in the nearest empty seat to the girl wearing the chain. There was one in the row behind her and slightly to her left. I slipped into it and studied the girl's profile. Her face was very still. She was smiling, but only just. Everybody else seemed to be laughing, but this girl looked as though she'd got a private joke. She was sitting very straight, and I got the impression that she was on her own. There was actually an empty place right beside her, but I didn't want to sit there. I wanted time to think what to do, and I also figured I might get a chance to see the S at close quarters to check out whether it really *was* an S or not.

After a couple of minutes I noticed that Leah was turning round in her seat, presumably looking for me. No wonder. I'd been gone for ages. I slid a little lower into my own seat to make sure that she didn't catch sight of me. Fortunately she turned back round again after a few seconds. I had to make something happen. But what? I considered climbing over and sitting in the empty seat next to the girl, but that idea still seemed stupid. She would think I was seriously weird. My brain was doing overtime trying to work out how to strike up a conversation.

The more I thought about it, the more ridiculous it seemed. I mean, the S probably stood for Sarah or Samantha – if there *was* an S in the first place. On the other hand the girl didn't look like a Sarah or a Samantha. She looked like the same type of person as Sid, only she was darker with shorter hair. It was the expression on her face that reminded me of Sid. There was a sort of toughness to it. I really wanted to talk to her and suddenly I knew what to do.

I leaned forward and spoke softly but clearly.

"Sid?" The girl turned abruptly and there was a moment while her eyes tried to adjust to the dark. "Sorry," I said, "I thought you were Sid. I just met her today. I joined the . . . oh . . . nothing."

The girl's eyes narrowed, then she gave me an uncertain half-smile. Out of the corner of my eye I could see Leah looking anxiously all round. I slid back down in my seat for a moment then, when the girl turned back to the film, I crept back into my proper place next to Leah.

"Where've you been? I've been really worried."

"Sorry, I felt sick."

"Are you OK?"

"Yeah."

"You're not really enjoying it, are you Andy?" Leah asked me in her typially sympathetic way.

"It's not my very best film ever," I admitted, being careful not to sound as though I was hating it, because I wasn't.

"We'll go and see your choice next time," replied Leah with a smile. She was always so fair about everything.

It was one big relief when the lights came up and we started to troop out. I wanted to tell Fen to look at the girl with the S round her neck on her way out, but I couldn't because she was deep in conversation with Jaimini and Tash. I deliberately hung back from the others, and as I passed the girl with the S, she said, "Do you know about the meeting tomorrow? It was only arranged this afternoon."

"Er, no, I didn't."

"Eleven o'clock. Usual place."

"I—" But she was already out of earshot. She had turned and walked all the way along the line of seats to approach the exit from the other side. My heart was beating as I rejoined the others in the foyer. I kept looking round but I didn't see the girl again. I don't think I would have recognized her even if I had seen her, because it had been so dark in the cinema.

The others all seemed full of laughter and lightness, and I didn't feel a part of it. The Strays seemed exciting and intriguing and I knew I had to join them. I also knew I had to tell the others, but not yet. I'd just tell Fen about seeing this girl with the S. That would be enough for now.

Jaimini

We felt very grown-up going back to the guest house in a taxi. The film had been absolutely brilliant. I was feeling quite sorry for Helen, who hadn't been able to go because of Peta. Poor Helen had actually given up an awful lot to make sure that us six could all get away for a few days' holiday. She's a really kind person. I made a resolution to look after Peta for a while the next day so Helen could go out.

When we got back Helen was still up. She was drinking coffee and brandy with Jules. Peta had gone to bed without any fuss apparently, and Helen seemed relaxed. She'd taken her shoes off and was resting her feet on Twister, the gnarled old dog.

"I think you're very misunderstood, aren't you?" I said in a soppy voice to the dozing animal. Then I jumped back with a shock, because for answer Twister gave me that same low growl that we'd heard the day before.

"The thing about Twister," explained Jules, "is that he knows exactly who he likes and who he doesn't. He makes an instant appraisal of all humans, and sticks rigidly to that first opinion. It doesn't matter how much you stroke him or sweet-talk him, Jaimini, you won't get anywhere now, I'm afraid."

"Don't worry, Jaimes, he didn't like me either," said Tash.

"Let's see if he likes me," said Luce, crouching down beside Twister. "Hello boy. I've got a dog at home. He's not quite as ugly as you, but for sheer hairiness I'm afraid he takes the biscuit."

Then Luce jumped up and squealed because Twister had suddenly snapped hard at her. The rest of us couldn't help laughing. It was such a human reaction of Twister's. Just as if he was saying, "Oh, get lost!"

"Huh! That's the last time I try to make friends with you!" said Luce in a very hurt voice that made us laugh even more. "Anyway, I don't like dogs that dribble," she added, turning her back on Twister and flopping into a chair with a magazine.

"Should *I* try?" asked Leah.

"Yes, you try Lee. Use different tactics from Luce, though," Tash said, leaning forward.

"I don't want to get bitten," said Lee, shrinking back a bit.

"No, don't worry, he never bites. He just shows his feelings by snapping and growling," Jules told us.

"All the same I think I'll keep my distance." So Leah went to the far side of the room and said, "Twister! Here boy!"

Twister took no notice, so Leah then inched forward calling his name in a singsong voice. On the fourth call, the weird dog deigned to raise his head and show her what he thought. The snap at Leah was even harder than the one at Luce, and again we all jumped a mile then collapsed in nervous giggles. We were more than a bit fazed by the crazy dog.

"Right, my turn!" said Fen. "I'm going to try something completely different. It's going to take courage!"

We watched Fen as she gulped a couple of times, presumably screwing up her courage. Then she marched over to Twister and ruffled his hair quite roughly. We all waited. My heart was really beating fast.

"You *are* quite sure he won't bite?" I double-checked with Jules.

"One hundred per cent certain," replied Jules.

Twister did absolutely nothing, as Fen kept stroking him quite roughly.

"What's that mean? Does he like me?" Fen asked Jules.

"I'm not sure. I think he's pretty indifferent, actually. But you've done the best so far because he doesn't *dis*like you."

"Well done, Fen!" we all said, breaking into applause as though she'd managed to tame a lion.

"What about Andy? Go on Andy, you have a go," I said.

"What?"

"See if Twister likes you."

For some reason or other Andy seemed very distracted. She appeared to be concentrating on something.

"My tactics are different again," she said, returning to earth. "My method is to do absolutely nothing and let him come to me if he wants to."

"Hey Andy! Playing hard to get?" asked Leah, giggling, while Helen and Jules laughed.

"Are you not particularly a dog person, Andy?" Jules asked her, eyeing her quizzically.

"She's a spy!" Luce informed Jules. "Spies don't have much time for dogs you see."

"I see."

"I'm tired. I think I'll go to bed," said Andy.

Fen

The moment Andy announced that she was going to bed, alarm bells rang. Andy simply didn't get tired. Out of all of us she had a reputation as the one who needed least sleep. About five different ideas flashed through my head. Andy wasn't really tired. She just wanted to get away. Maybe she wanted to talk to me. Come to think of it, she'd been in a world of her own ever since the end of the film. Had something happened when she'd gone out to the loo?

"I'm pretty tired too," I quickly said. Andy's expression didn't change, but she was subtle. She'd never make it obvious what she was up to.

"Me too," said Tash. "Come on, let's all go to bed, then we'll feel like getting up early tomorrow and we can have as much of the day as possible to have a good time."

"Good thinking," said Jaimini, jumping up. I glanced at Andy. This time I knew I was right. She was trying not to look hacked off, because now she'd lost the chance to talk to me in private.

As the others said goodnight to Helen and Jules and began to troop out, Andy said, "I couldn't have a drink, could I?"

"Yes, of course," said Jules jumping up. "What do you want?"

"No, it's all right. I'll make it."

"Oh me too, please," I said, following Andy through to the kitchen. I was holding my breath, praying that the others weren't following. I expected Andy was doing the same. Unfortunately we were out of luck.

"Hot chocolate! Yum!" came Luce's voice just behind us.

"It doesn't take three of us to make the hot chocolate," I said, in a sudden burst of inspiration. I gave Luce a pleading look. "You're the best at hot-chocolate-making, Luce."

"Flattery will get you everywhere," Luce replied. It was obvious that she was pleased. "Three hot chocolates coming up," she said. "Go on you two. Off you go. I'm in charge."

So Andy and I went off. Jules and Helen were still in the sitting room and the others were upstairs. Luce was in the kitchen, so that only left the big breakfast room where Andy and I could talk. Without a word spoken we both headed in that direction, shutting the door softly behind us.

"What is it, Andy?" I whispered. "And why all the secrecy? You'd better tell me quickly. Luce makes hot chocolate at the speed of light."

"I saw this girl in the cinema," Andy launched straight in. "She had an S dangling from a chain round her neck. I was so curious about whether she was one of the Strays that I pretended I thought she was Sid. I wanted her to know that I knew about the Strays, so that she knew I could be trusted, but on the other hand, I knew I mustn't say the name 'Strays', in case she was nothing to do with them. I said that I knew Sid and that I'd joined the – And then I stopped and said, 'Oh, nothing.'"

"Oh Andy! You haven't, though!"

"Haven't what?"

"Joined anything. You gave her the wrong impression."

"I know, but it was all I could think of saying. And then I had to get back to you lot. But when we went out at the end of the film I hung back. And when I passed her seat she asked me if I knew about the meeting tomorrow. She said it was at eleven o'clock at the usual place." Andy paused and looked at me, her eyes lighting up with a look I recognized. "Let's go, Fen, and see what the Strays are all about, before we join. Otherwise we might never get the chance to go to a meeting. They might only hold them once a week."

"I bet tomorrow's meeting has been specially called by Sid to tell the others about us," I said.

"We don't have to let anyone see us. It's just that we've no idea what we're getting ourselves into here, and I'd like to check it out without them knowing."

I was getting quite alarmed about Andy. She was sounding pretty obsessed by the Strays and it wasn't Andy's style to be obsessed about things. She'd shocked me with all that she'd said. It was incredible that she'd seen someone with an S so soon. Unless that girl had been deliberately following us. It was all beginning to feel quite spooky, but also really mysterious and exciting. Irresistible, in fact. I realized I'd caught the same bug that Andy had. There was no time to talk about all that, though. We had to get on with making a plan for the next day. I hadn't said anything about the Strays to the others earlier on, for Andy's sake, but now I realized that I felt the same. It suddenly seemed quite important to keep it to ourselves, for a while at least.

"How shall we get away from the others tomorrow?"

"Same as last time. We all go out to the centre quite early. Then at roughly half past ten one of us suggests going to the cafe. Then after twenty minutes or so, I say I'm going for a quick run, and you say you'll come with me."

"OK."

There wasn't time for even another word because the door opened and in came Jules.

"Oh! What are you two doing in here?"

"We just came in to see what the breakfast room looked like. Then we got talking," Andy said calmly.

"So what do you think?" Jules asked.

"It's lovely and big. Is the guest house usually full?" I asked.

"Depends on the time of year. For some unknown reason the Easter holidays are the most popular time of all."

We chatted a bit more with Jules then went off upstairs to bed, exchanging "that-was-a-close-one" looks on the way.

The hot chocolate made me sleepy and I felt myself dropping off as soon as I'd finished it, which was probably a good thing. Andy and I needed to get everybody up nice and early the next day.

Chapter 6

Tash

Just when I was really dying to talk to Fen she fell asleep. It wasn't that I wanted to talk about anything in particular, simply that I would have been more comfortable if someone was awake with me in case those noises started again. I shut my eyes and thought nice thoughts, but I wasn't getting at all tired.

Then it started. The first bump was the most terrifying. It made me sit bolt upright in bed. I stayed there hardly breathing as other little bumps started. It was impossible to tell where all the noises were coming from. I was desperate to wake Fen up so she could listen too, but I thought that would be cruel. Then I weighed up the idea of waking Mum up but Peta would be sure to wake up really early in the morning so Mum wouldn't want to be disturbed at both ends of the night. Anyway, that was babyish. I mean, what would I do if Mum wasn't here? No, I had to cope on my own somehow.

The taps seemed to be coming in groups, so I thought I'd count how many there were in each. The first time I counted there were eight, the next, nine, and the next, twenty. Then there was only one loud tap all on its own.

Maybe that was the end of the tapping. After all, it had started with one loud one, so perhaps it would finish like that, too. Suddenly I wanted it to stop. It was too scary. I decided to go to the loo and hoped that when I got back it would have stopped. So I did, and when I crept back into the bedroom a minute later, all seemed to be quiet, so I slipped back into bed and held my breath for ages, until I felt that I could relax again.

As I lay there, unable to sleep, something suddenly occurred to me. Perhaps the number of taps in each group had a meaning, like a code. So if there were eight taps in the first group, that could be the letter H, which would make the group of nine taps I, and the group of twenty T. What did that spell? Hit! I almost shot out of bed when I realized what it spelt. Hit what? What was the message supposed to mean? Then there was the tap at the end. So if that was A, it was saying "Hit a. . ." Whatever could it be? Suddenly I wished I hadn't left the room. Then I would have heard the rest of the message. As it was I would have to wait till the next night. In fact, I might have lost my chance altogether. I smiled to myself in the dark. It was funny how I'd completely changed my mind about the taps. I'd been so scared a few minutes before and now I was filled with curiosity and excitement. Maybe this was going to turn out to be a personal message for me. I decided not to tell anyone. This was going to be my secret. There was no way I could get to sleep after that, so I read my book, and the next thing I knew, Fen was shaking me, trying to wake me up.

"Tash, it's eight o'clock. Wake up."

"Didn't get to sleep," I managed to mumble.

"What? You didn't get to sleep?"

"Mm," was all I could be bothered to say.

"But it's eight o'clock. You were going to get up early to make the day as long as possible. Remember?"

I *did* remember, but it didn't seem to matter any more. All that mattered was that I stayed asleep for as long as possible. I didn't even answer Fen. I just hoped that she might realize I'd changed my mind and that I wanted to be left alone. But she was determined to wake me up.

"Come on Tash. I'll bring you a nice cup of tea and some toast. OK?

"Mm," I replied noncommittally, and she rushed off.

Andy

Something was wrong. I thought I was awake but I must still have been dreaming. I couldn't move. Well, that wasn't strictly true. I managed to move my toes and one of my arms. I could turn my head from side to side. But the rest of my body was weighted down. All I could think was that I must have been in the middle of my worst nightmare. Yet I knew I wasn't. I opened my eyes and saw the daylight filtering in through the curtains, little blobs of light and shadows running across the ceiling. I turned my head. Leah was fast asleep. The door was wide open and I still couldn't move. This was serious. My head shot up and I got the shock of my life. There, lying on top of me in a heavy, floppy heap with one eye open, leering at me, was Twister. He weighed a ton.

"Get off me, dog," I said in a long-suffering voice, because now I knew I wasn't paralyzed I couldn't be bothered to be cross. There were more important things on my mind, and I wanted this big beast off me so I could get up.

On seeing that I'd woken up and was apparently address-ing his lordship himself, Twister licked my face as though it was a bowl of water in the middle of the desert. Then he turned round and round and round on me in tight little circles, pressing his paws into my stomach without a care in the world. So this was how he'd got his name, was it?

"Leah!" I called gently. "Look at this!"

There was no reply from Leah. She was sound asleep.

"Get off me Twister!" But Twister had other plans. He was trying to get into the Guinness Book of Records for doing more turns on a human being than any other dog in history.

"Andy! Where did Twister spring from?" It was Fen at the door.

"I don't know. I'm not sure that springing is in his repertoire, actually. I think he's decided to specialize in twisting."

Fen laughed and called Twister, but he just ignored her. "Jules was right, wasn't she? He decides who he likes and who he doesn't and he sticks to it. Poor Andy. He's besotted with you, probably because you played hard to get. It's no good me calling him off because he's indifferent to me."

"Can you get Peta, Fen? He loves her too."

So Fen rushed off to get Peta, who, of course, thought it was brilliant fun. She'd been trying to wake Helen up, but Helen didn't want to be disturbed and was apparently delighted when Fen relieved her of Peta.

"Come on you silly old Twister," said Peta, clambering on the bed too, which made me feel positively claustrophobic. Twister was in ecstasy. He licked Peta then he licked me then he turned a few more times. Even when he barked with pleasure it didn't wake Leah up, though.

"Can you get him off me, Peta? Go and stand by the door then call him. Go on. That's a good girl. Are the others awake, Fen?"

"I'll go and see."

"Twister! Twister! Come here, you silly ole doggy-woggy."

Eventually the enormous weight flopped to the floor and did its twisting act in the centre of the room with Peta rushing round and round too.

"It's like a circus in here," said Fen, returning from Luce and Jaimini's room. "Sorry," she added, "they're both asleep."

"We'll have to change the plan," I whispered, glancing at Leah to check she was still asleep too. "We'll set off before they wake up. We'll leave a note."

So Fen and I got dressed as quickly as possible, praying that the others wouldn't wake up after all. We didn't bother with breakfast. Peta was the only problem. She wanted to know where we were going. And she desperately wanted to come with us, even getting herself dressed and saying that she wasn't hungry and didn't want breakfast.

"We'll be far too fast for you, Peta, because we're going to run," I explained gently.

"And your mummy will be sad if she wakes up and finds you've gone out already," Fen added, scraping the barrel for reasons why Peta couldn't possibly come with us. Actually, we both felt really sorry for her, but there was no way she could come too.

We'd just convinced her that Jules would probably want to give Twister a bath (that was a burst of inspiration on Fen's part) when into the kitchen came a very bleary-eyed Jaimini and Luce.

"You two are up early."

"We thought we'd go for a walk."

"Wait for us. We'll come too," said Jaimini.

"Yeah, and the others are awake now. Let's have some breakfast then all go out for a walk. It's a lovely day. Cold and crisp. Blue sky and sunshine."

"Since when did you turn into a weather reporter?" Jaimini asked Luce.

"Actually, Andy and I have been awake for ages," Fen tried. "We really wanted to get going."

"We'll be ever so quick," said Luce and she shot back upstairs to speed the others up. There was nothing for it. We had to go back to plan A.

Leah

I was the last to wake up, and it took me ages to remember where I was. Everyone else was already up, dressed and discussing what to do with the day. Helen was trying to be diplomatic and let us go off on our own, but Jaimini insisted that Helen should come with us, because otherwise she'd be stuck looking after Peta again. Peta was desperate to come along with us and also to bring Twister along, too. Jules said she thought we'd find him a pain after a bit, but we decided to take him anyway, for Peta's sake. Helen said that if we wanted we could all take a bus to a place where there were some fantastic caves where they mined a stone called Blue John. Apparently in one of the caves you went down loads and loads of steps. Then, because it was so narrow, you had to go along the bottom of the cave in a boat. I thought it sounded scary but I knew Andy would be really keen to go.

"The caves sound fantastic, Helen. I'd love to go," said Luce.

"I've been reading about them in the guidebook and the little town that's nearby sounds lovely, too," said Jamini. "There'll be all sorts of jewellery in the shops there, Luce. We can buy some souvenirs."

"Yeah, it'll be great, won't it?" Luce said, smiling round at the rest of us. We were all keen except Andy and Fen, surprisingly.

"I thought you'd really love to go down the Blue John mines, Andy," said Helen, looking a bit hurt.

"Yes I would – normally. It's just that it's such a beautiful day, and I'd like to make the most of the sunshine. I don't suppose we could possibly go to the caves tomorrow, could we?"

"What do the rest of you want to do?" Helen asked.

"I don't mind at all what we do," said Tash.

"Well, there are some lovely walks in here," continued Helen, flipping through the guidebook. "Long walks, short walks, walks with picnics. . ."

"Picnic! Picnic!" shouted Peta. "I want picnic!"

"Yes, that would be lovely," Jaimini and Tash agreed.

"I was wondering if we could go back to the town centre for a little while, then go for a walk later," Fen said, and Andy immediately agreed.

"Yes, then you could buy that ballet book you saw," she said to Fen.

I think that was the moment that I first thought something was going on with those two, but I'd no idea what. It even crossed my mind that they'd come across a couple of boys the previous day when they'd gone off on their own, because they'd hardly said a word about what they'd been doing. Come to think of it, that would explain why Andy had taken so long to go to the loo in the cinema. She'd said she felt sick, but Andy never felt sick. Maybe she was having a secret meeting with a boy in the foyer. No. That wasn't like Andy at all. Boyfriends didn't interest her. She'd got her special French friend Jacques, but he was the only boy she'd ever given two pence for, apart from her ordinary friends who were boys.

"Right," said Helen, "let's go into town this morning, then we'll have lunch in that cafe you told me about. After that we could go for a walk in the Dales. Good. Decision made. Let's get going."

When we arrived in the centre of town, Helen suggested that we meet up at the bottom of the escalator at about twelve-thirty for lunch. Jaimini and Luce said that they would take Peta so Helen could have a break, and Helen seemed really grateful.

"There's a lovely cafe in the basement," Jaimini said. "Do you remember, Tash? It's got beautiful plants and trellises and lovely low lights."

"Yes, it's really atmospheric," Tash agreed.

"Fine," said Helen. "Lunch among the plants and the low lights, then."

So off we went our separate ways. Helen went straight up the escalator. Luce, Jaimini and Peta went off towards a toy shop on the ground floor. Fen asked Andy if she wanted to go to the sports shop and Andy said she'd love to. So that left Tash and me. I didn't care what I did or who I was with. All I wanted to do was to keep my eyes open for that boy I'd seen. If only that horrible waitress hadn't worked in the cafe, I'd probably have suggested going back there, but apart from Andy, everyone would think I was off my rocker if I tried that, after our dreadful experience yesterday.

Tash

Leah was in a strange, dreamy sort of mood. Maybe this was her holiday mode: I'd certainly never seen her like this before. She didn't seem to be able to make a decision about anything. I didn't mind, though, because it was good fun just strolling about without a care in the world. We went in and out of shop after shop at breakneck speed. I'd never seen Leah with so much nervous energy. She just seemed to want to cover as much ground as possible, but the funny thing was that when we were actually in the shops, she hardly looked at anything at all, she just moved from one section to another, always looking ahead to the next place or the next shop, as though she was searching for something or someone. Weird!

After tearing around about seven or eight shops like this, we walked through the precinct, heading towards the main road.

"I wish Emma didn't work in that cafe," Leah said after a while, "because I really liked it in there. Didn't you?"

"Yes, it was OK."

"I just feel like a coke or something, don't you?"

"Er, well, yeah, but not in there."

"No. Right."

Leah was acting very strangely, but I couldn't question her about her odd behaviour, because it was suddenly impossible to speak. We'd come out of the precinct and were walking along the main road when there was the most earth-shattering roaring noise that made us both block our ears instinctively. A motorbike was zooming past us with the driver dressed all in black. He was going at top speed and making a noise like a rocket.

"Ouch!" yelled Leah, jumping back as if she'd been stung.

I didn't grasp what had happened at first. I just stared, as if mesmerized, after the bike, as it roared away into the distance, leaving Leah and me standing in our own little patch of stunned silence, with a medium-sized brown parcel at our feet. We both stared at the parcel and then slowly looked around us. People seemed to be going about their everyday business as though nothing at all had happened.

"Did you see that?" asked Leah, pointing after the bike and still looking rather dazed, as though expecting a crowd to flock round her at any moment.

"Did it hit you, Lee?"

"Yes. Look!" she said, turning her big eyes to the parcel, still at her feet, as though it was personally responsible for hurting her. "It just flew off the bike. Just like that!"

I bent down and picked up the square package. It wasn't very heavy, but I could imagine that it must have hurt because it had flown off at such a speed.

"Mrs Sherwood, forty-eight Silverlands—" I started to read.

"Never mind that. What about my hip?" Leah suddenly said, which wasn't like Leah at all.

"Oh sorry. Are you all right?"

"I'd better not investigate right here, but I bet I'm going to have multicoloured bruises round my hip bone. It really whacked me."

"Do you think the driver chucked it off himself?" I asked, my imagination filling up with all sorts of ideas about stolen packages.

"Omigod! It may be a bomb!" squealed Leah. "Drop it Tash! Quick!"

"I'm sure it's not, and it just dropped off by mistake, but it's odd that nobody's taking a blind bit of notice, except us two."

It was true that there weren't all that many people about, because we'd come quite a distance from the precinct without really noticing, but all the same, I thought that someone might have been curious about a motorbike going at the speed of sound and leaving parcels strewn in its wake.

"What shall we do with it?" I asked Leah.

"Take it to the police?"

"The police? Why?" And then I realized that Leah was still seriously thinking that it might be something dangerous.

"If it's a bomb, Leah, I don't think it would be a very good idea to take it anywhere. But don't worry, I'm certain it's something perfectly ordinary."

"I'm sure you're right. I mean, why should poor Mrs Sherwood get picked on to be blown up?"

Leah's eyebrows were knitted together in that worried look that we're all used to seeing on her face. I suddenly came up with the perfect idea to make her relax.

"I know, let's deliver it ourselves!"

"No, we can't. Even if it's not a bomb, it might be something else dangerous."

"Look, Leah, I reckon that the man on the motorbike was one of those couriers who deliver letters and parcels for people who want a speedier service than the post, and he was going so fast that this one fell off. Simple!"

"And I reckon that he's a member of a secret anti-government organization, trying to destroy the world," Leah said stubbornly.

"Pretty silly way of going about it," I pointed out, and that brought a smile to Leah's face as she realized that she was getting worried for no real reason.

"OK, you win," she said. "Let's go back to that town plan that we passed when we came out of the precinct and see if we can spot Silverlands on it."

A couple of minutes later we were jumping up and down with excitement because we'd found Silverlands on the map, and it didn't look very far away at all.

"Come on, let's go," I said. "Just think how pleased Mrs Sherwood is going to be when she realizes her precious parcel isn't lost after all."

"She might not have given the parcel a thought. She might be just sitting quietly at home, not even knowing a parcel is on its way for her."

"That's a point. Do you think we ought to phone first?"

Leah was just pondering this when I spotted a phone box across the road.

"That's fate," I announced. "Come on, let's go and get the number from directory inquiries.

"Hello, I'm sorry to disturb you," I said in my most adult voice a few moments later, "but is this Mrs Sherwood of forty-eight Silverlands?"

"Yes, it is," said the very surprised-sounding lady at the other end of the line.

"Well, the thing is, my friend and I were just walking along when a parcel with your name and address on it flew off the back of a motorbike."

There was a long pause and I wondered whether the line had gone dead.

"Is this a joke?" the voice finally said.

"No, no, honestly. We've got your parcel here."

Again there was a pause and then, when Mrs Sherwood spoke the next time, her voice was soft and worried-sounding. I had to strain to hear what she was saying.

"What size is the parcel?"

"It's about as big as a big box of tissues, but heavier than that. Do you want us to bring it round to you?"

Again she hesitated. "Er, well, if you're nearby."

"Yes we are."

"Right then."

"We'll be about five minutes."

"Yes, but don't—"

I'll never know what she was going to say then, because my money ran out and we were cut off.

"What did she say?" Leah wanted to know.

"She sounded very mysterious."

"She's probably suspicious of us. I mean, if you look at it from her point of view, it must seem most peculiar."

"Oh well, we'd better deliver it now I've said that we're going to."

So off we went, both beginning to wish that we'd never got involved. Silverlands was a cul-de-sac with loads of modern houses in it. They didn't all look the same, but they did all look smart and neat and new. Number forty-eight had very clean windows, a dark-green front door and a gleaming gold knocker.

"Here goes!" I said, knocking and then standing back.

An extremely glamorous-looking woman opened the door cautiously, gave Leah and I a quick, nervous smile, then took the parcel that I was holding out and studied the hand-writing as though her life depended on it. Something must have clicked into place, because the expression on her face suddenly changed completely and she looked overcome with emotion, sort of happy yet worried all at once. When she spoke it was in a whisper.

"Thanks very much. Very kind of you."

"Who is it?" came a gruff, deep voice from somewhere behind her. All the happiness left the woman's face, so that only the anxiety remained.

"Just someone wanting directions," she called over her shoulder. "Thanks very much," she repeated in a whisper to us, then, with trembling hands, she passed the parcel back to me. "Could you leave it behind that shrub when you go?" There was something in her manner that made me think it was urgent that we set off immediately, and I was right, because a second later the door was pulled back roughly and a thin man wearing a scowl appear behind the woman. Quick as a flash I hid the parcel behind my back. Leah and I must have had the same thought at exactly the same moment, because she stood behind me and took the parcel, which meant that I could bring my hands round to the front and not look as though I was hiding something. Goodness knows what made Leah and I react so quickly. Maybe it was the look of panic on the woman's face.

"And it's on the left at the top," Mrs Sherwood said in a very normal voice, as though she'd just finished giving us directions.

"Right, thank you very much then," I said. "We'll be off."

The man continued to stare, but the woman gave me a very grateful smile. That just left the problem of Leah and I turning round without the parcel being noticed. I needn't have worried, because the door shut immediately, so we turned and scuttled away in silence.

"We're supposed to put it behind the shrub," Leah hissed

at me out of the corner of her mouth as I strode down the drive.

"I know, but he may be watching out of the window. I didn't like the look of him one little bit. Let's go down the road and come back in a minute."

So off we walked, probably looking very stiff and strange, because it was impossible to relax thinking that someone might be spying on us out of a window.

"I do hope we're not being watched," said Leah in a funny, croaky voice.

"Why?"

"Because I'm about to burst out laughing."

"Well you mustn't."

"I won't be able to help it. I can feel it coming. It's because I'm nervous."

"Right, you keep walking and I'll nip back and hide the parcel."

So that's what happened. My heart was beating wildly because I thought that any second the front door of number forty-eight would fly open and that grumpy-looking man would cry out, "A-ha! Caught you!" But there was no sign of anyone at any of the windows, so I just put the package behind the shrub as fast as I could, and then made a dash for it.

As I caught up with Leah, who was out of Silverlands by then, I realized that she was gesturing wildly, trying to tell me something. It looked as though she was pointing at something behind me. I turned round, and there, running towards me, was Mrs Sherwood.

"Sorry love. I thought I was going to miss you," she said, gasping for breath.

"I put the parcel behind the shrub," I explained. "I didn't do it straight away, in case—"

"Yes, yes, I know. I saw you. I didn't come about that. I came to thank you both. You'll never know how helpful you've been today. It's for his birthday, you see, and it's vital that he doesn't know about it till the actual day. So I've got to keep it a secret."

She was smiling from one to the other of us and personally I didn't believe a word she was saying. She'd not looked to me like a loving wife, organizing a big surprise for her husband. All the same, I couldn't really say anything, so I just smiled, said, "Oh, right," and tried to look as though I went round hiding parcels behind shrubs for complete strangers on a regular basis, so it was no big deal for me.

"Anyway my dears, I wanted to give you a little something by way of a reward for your kindness and thoughtfulness, because I can tell you for nothing, there aren't many young lasses around these parts who'd put themselves out for a stranger. Mind you, you're not from round here, are you?"

"No, we're on holiday for a few days," I explained.

"Well, here's a bit of spending money for you. It won't go far these days, but it's better than nothing, isn't it?"

She handed me a ten-pound note.

"Are you sure?" I asked, which was a silly thing to say because she wasn't going to snatch it back and say, "No sorry, changed my mind."

"I'm very sure," she replied, patting my hand. "Very sure indeed," she added, pressing the money into my palm. "And thank you again."

Then she turned and strolled back to the house, head held high, as though she'd been acting one part, and now she was getting into another role.

We called out our thanks and set off back to the centre to meet the others.

83

"What a weird adventure," said Leah, turning to me with shining eyes the moment the woman was out of earshot.

"Can't wait to tell the others," I agreed, and we instinctively broke into a jog. All the way back we took turns guessing what the real reason for the secrecy was, because Leah, like me, hadn't believed the birthday-present story. Each reason we thought of got more and more outlandish, and in the end we'd invented a whole tale of political espionage surrounding the couple.

In the restaurant with the plants and the low lights we told our story in graphic and dramatic detail. As we spoke, the others listened open-mouthed.

"You lucky things!" said Luce, as I flashed the ten-pound note around.

"Let's spend it on scratch cards," Leah suggested. I thought that was a great idea and Mum went off to get them. She came back with a bag of sweets for Peta and thirteen scratch cards because she'd put some extra money to the ten pounds. So we all had two scratch cards each and Mum had one for herself. There was silence for a minute or so while we scratched away, and then a big shriek went up from Mum, who had won ten pounds.

"Oh no!" she wailed. "This should be Tash and Leah's winnings by rights."

"No, it doesn't matter," said Leah. "It was our idea to share it."

"Well, this is what I'm going to do," said Mum. "Tash and Leah get two pounds fifty each, the rest of us one pound each. I'll buy another load of scratch cards and if anyone wins this time, they get to keep the money."

So that's what we did and nobody won a penny, but we all agreed that it had been great fun anyway! We never did get to the bottom of the secret parcel mystery, but Luce was absolutely convinced that the man on the bike was some kind of superhero who was having a passionate affair with Mrs Sherwood. And who knows, she may have been right!

Chapter 7

Luce

"So what shall we do then?" I asked Jaimini the moment we all split up and went our separate ways. But it was little Peta in her buggy who thought I was after her own particular brand of expert advice.

"We do playing games," she informed us gleefully.

"No we do not," I replied firmly. "Let's ask Auntie Jaimini what we're going to do, shall we?"

"I'm not her auntie. And I don't mind what we do. How about a bit of shopping?"

I wrinkled up my nose. I'd had a brief look round the day before. I'd got less spending money than anyone else as far as I could make out. So what was new? The others had always been better than me at saving money. "Let's compromise and do a couple of shops."

"What's a cupplashop?" asked Peta twisting round in her buggy. "Is it nice cream?"

"No it's not. It's—"

"Peta wants ve loo."

"Are you sure you can't wait for a few minutes?"

"It might come out and go all over ve buggy and all over ve road and all over the whole world wiv all the

86

peoples in it. And ven vay'd all be wet, like it's raining, and—"

"Yes, OK Peta, I think we've got the idea," said Jaimini, who was pushing the buggy briskly in the direction of the nearest loos, which were in the basement next to the cafe. "We must have been mad volunteering to take Peta," she added in a softer voice.

The loo trip took ages, largely because Peta insisted that she wanted both Jaimini *and* me in the loo with her. I was surprised she didn't want the buggy as well. Jaimini kept on saying that we must be firm with her and not let her get her own way on everything, so we told her that there was only room for one other person in the loo with her, and that person would be me, but she kicked up such a fuss and made so much noise about it that it got embarrassing, so Jaimes went in instead. Well, that didn't help at all, which was why we gave in in the end, telling her she was a very naughty girl while secretly thinking that she was a very clever girl indeed to be able to wrap two thirteen-year-olds round her little finger.

"Right, from now on, we're not going to give in to anything," said Jaimes, "even if she screams the place down and attracts a crowd of thousands."

"I quite agree," I said, feeling just as determined as Jaimes as we headed for a wonderful big rug shop. Though it sold mainly rugs, it also had cushions, towels, baskets, candles and all the things that Jaimes absolutely loves for sale. She couldn't resist buying a wall-hanging for her bedroom. It was when we were leaving this shop that Jaimes suddenly elbowed me in the ribs. I was completely used to getting elbowed like this because it was Jaimes's way of stopping me from putting my foot in it, which I did on a pretty regular basis. But this time I felt sure there was no way I was doing anything wrong.

"What?" I asked her.

For answer she just nodded towards the shop immediately opposite, and I saw what she meant. We could clearly see Helen just inside the door talking to a man. "So what?" you might say, but this was *serious* talking. You see, Tash has always been quite keen on the idea of having a stepfather, and every so often a likely candidate turns up, but somehow or other, they're never quite right, or it turns out that while the six of us have all been fondly imagining that Helen is seeing some man, they're actually just friends or colleagues.

"It's probably nothing," said Jaimini quickly. "We mustn't jump to conclusions. We're always wrong."

"We're not wrong this time," I breathed, because Helen and the man were looking into each other's eyes as though the rest of the world didn't exist. Quite honestly I think the three of us could have gone and danced a naked jig round them and they wouldn't have noticed.

"Go! Go! Go now!" said Peta, subtly hinting at what she wanted to do. She hadn't spotted her mother, fortunately. So off we went, out of the centre and out of the precinct, heading towards a part of the town that we'd never seen before.

"Let's forget all about it," said Jaimini. "It's none of our business, after all."

"What, you mean let's not tell the others?" I asked, feeling excited that we had a secret all to ourselves. Jaimini nodded and we grinned at each other.

We had taken a turning and were going through a sort of alleyway alongside the back of a huge hotel that was cleverly built into a crescent. It was really beautiful, a very grand and decorative building in stone that had a sort of rusty-pink tinge to it. Peta was running her hand along the wall as we went. If she hadn't been wearing gloves she would have scraped the skin off because the stone was natural and rough. Jaimini thought the building was probably from the early nineteenth century. Goodness knows how she knew that. Well, I *do* know, actually. It's got something to do with the fact that she pays attention during history lessons. I'm determined to try that one day.

"Hot!" said Peta.

"No, it's not," I answered.

"Maybe she's building up friction, so it feels as though the wall is hot," said Jaimini, just to prove that she also pays attention during science lessons.

"Hot. It *is*!" insisted Peta. So we stopped and felt the wall ourselves. Peta was right. There were two or three stones that were quite warm, so we decided to stop and press ourselves against them. Peta was too small, but she got out of the buggy and pretended that she, too, was huddling into the heat instead of leaning against a cold bit.

"Come on then, Jaimes. Why is it hot?"

"Probably because there's a boiler or something just behind here."

"Maybe it's the hotel kitchen," I suggested.

"Yes, could be," Jaimini agreed, which made me feel as though I was up there with the big brains. Then we all jumped because somebody spoke, and it was just as though the person was right next to us, yet there was no one in sight.

"In with the next batch," said the voice.

"Who's vat?" Peta called as she jumped dramatically into

the middle of the alleyway and tipped her head jerkily from left to right like a little bird. Two men laughed on the other side of the wall, and Jaimini pointed to an air vent that was very low down.

"Their voices are carrying through there," she whispered, with a giggle.

"What you laughin' at?" asked Peta in a very big voice, her eyes wide, her little body facing the wall now she'd sussed that was where the voices were coming from.

"Hello. What's your name?" asked one of the men in a voice he'd obviously put on specially for talking to little kids. He sounded very nice, and Jaimes and I didn't think for a moment that there was anything to worry about. Yes, he was a stranger, but he *was* on the other side of a stone wall.

Peta had now realized that maybe the voice was making its way to her through the vent, so she crouched down in front of it and said, "Peta. What's yours?"

There was more laughter from the other side of the wall, and Jaimini and I kept quiet because we didn't want to cramp Peta's style. It was all so funny. I wished I'd had a video camera because Peta had decided that crouching wasn't good enough and she was lying on her tummy with her mouth really close to the air vent.

"She'll be getting her clothes all filthy," said Jaimini.

"It'll brush off when it's dry," I whispered, quoting something that Mum often seemed to say, but not really knowing if it was true in this case.

"Are you all on your own, Peta?" asked the voice.

"No," Peta answered.

"Are you with your mum or your dad?" asked the voice.

"No. Are you?"

More laughter from the other side of the wall. Jaimini

and I exchanged "Shall we?" looks, then I spoke, crouching down and speaking clearly.

"Peta's not on her own. My friend and I are looking after her."

"Her! I thought it was a boy."

"No, you spell it P-E-T-A." I turned to Jaimini and whispered, "I must be going mad talking to a wall!"

"Got to go now, Mister Wall," said Peta in her big voice, which made the men on the other side crack up.

"How old are you, Peta?" asked the other man.

"Free. How old are you?"

"Much older than that," came the reply.

"How old are you Janey?" Peta asked Jaimini in a whisper. She always called her Janey.

"Thirteen," whispered back Jaimes.

"And Janey and Lucy Goosey are fifteen, right?"

"Right," replied one of them. "Well, have a nice day."

"Bye-bye Mister Wall and ve uvver Mister Wall," Peta said politely.

"Actually it's Stan and Tom," they answered.

"No snot. Smister Wall and ve uvver Mister Wall," Peta calmly corrected them as she got back in her buggy and stuck her thumb in her mouth. She was obviously bored with poor Stan and Tom, who were making such an effort for her. Either that or she didn't want anything to spoil the idea of talking to a wall.

"Bye" called Jaimini and I, as we went on our way.

"Bye", came the friendly reply.

The more we thought about what had just happened, the more ridiculously funny it seemed. By the time we'd got back to the centre, we were creased up laughing and Peta was getting cross, telling us to stop being silly girls. We bought ice creams and walked along eating them. Big mistake. Peta got more ice cream down her front than she did in her mouth, so we had to make another trip to the loo to get her cleaned up a bit before meeting the others.

Andy

Fen and I couldn't help feeling nervous as we made our way towards the park, Twister trotting obediently at our side. It had finally been decided that the daft dog should be allowed to come out with us and have some fun. Peta had got fed up with him pulling all the time, so we'd decided to take over as we knew we were going to the park.

"How can we be sure that the meeting will take place in the park, Andy?"

"We can't be sure of anything. In fact, I very much doubt that it *will* be in the park. It's too open for one thing. I just figured it was the logical place to start looking."

"Don't you think Sid might be a bit cross about us showing up at a meeting place when we're not even members?"

"We've just got to make sure we're not seen by anyone."

"How can you be so calm about it all, Andy?"

"I'm not calm, I'm worried. But you know me: once I decide to do something I've got to do it." I looked at Fen's pale frowning face and suddenly felt sorry for her. "Look Fen, I don't mind if you want me to go on my own. Honestly. You could easily find one of the others if you go back now."

"No, it's OK, I'm not that chicken," Fen said with a slightly shaky smile. "I'll come with you."

I couldn't get over how good Twister was being. Until

now he'd been dragging everyone round at about a hundred miles per hour and suddenly darting off to places where he wasn't supposed to be going, or getting his lead wrapped round some poor unsuspecting person's legs. He was such a strange dog, one minute stubborn and lazy, the next totally hyper, but right now he was being as good as gold.

It didn't take us long to get to the park and we were more or less bang on time, but there was not a soul in sight and the whole place had a very desolate feel to it. Even the children's play area, although full of exciting things to do, was drab and grey. The wind felt cold and the sky looked pale and harsh. I wondered if snow was on its way.

"Shall we go and wait in the little house?" Fen suggested. But Twister had other ideas. We had let him off the lead and he was crashing about the park like a lion in the wild.

"Twister!" I shouted, but he ignored me.

"Twister!" yelled Fen at the top of her voice, but he ignored her, too.

"Never mind, he's enjoying himself. Let's leave him to play," I suggested.

"What if he gets lost or deliberately runs away?"

Twister was still in sight, however, so we didn't panic, just headed in his direction while keeping our eyes open for anybody who might be waiting for the meeting. The trouble was, there was absolutely no one anywhere in sight. At the far end of the park was a huge mass of trees. They were conifers, so they hadn't shed their leaves. Twister was trotting round as though he really wasn't sure what to make of them.

"Twister!" shouted Fen as she chucked a stick that she'd picked up earlier on. "Go on boy! Go fetch!" Twister saw the branch and looked as though he could be persuaded to run and fetch it, but then suddenly changed his mind and returned to his trotting-along-by-the-trees exercise.

"Something's caught his interest in there. I wonder what it is," I said, my imagination moving into second gear.

"Maybe it's a rotten tomato or something equally exciting to dogs," said Fen, without too much interest.

"Maybe it's the wreckage of a helicopter crash," I suggested.

"Perhaps it's a UFO and those trees are full of aliens," said Fen, warming to the theme.

"Yes, a space capsule with aliens, not only from another planet, but from another time zone!" I went on, my voice instinctively dropping to a whisper as we got within a few metres of the trees.

"Yes, or maybe it's a lady dog!" Fen said, which made us completely crack up, only silently, so as not to let the scary aliens know we were there!

"Come on Twister, go find the nice lady dog," Fen joked, while Twister watched us and wagged his tail.

The trees were set very close together, with low, thick branches that let through no light.

"Shall we go in and see?" asked Fen, "Or shall we go back to the centre?"

Part of me felt the same sort of anxiety that Fen obviously felt, but the other part (the stronger part) had to investigate, so with beating hearts we began our walk into the darkness. Even the snow hadn't managed to penetrate this eerie dark-green and brown place. There were pine needles on the ground, thousands of them, and we trod gingerly with Twister just ahead of us, leading the way.

After only a few steps we stopped and hissed at Twister to come to heel. He stopped too, but didn't come back to us. We listened hard: voices, whispering. Fen put her hand on my arm as my gaze tried to penetrate the trees. "Look," I whispered. "There are lights flickering." As if mesmerized, we both began to follow the lights, Twister still just ahead.

"I'm scared," Fen said. "There's definitely someone in there." She stood rooted to the ground while I went on, with Twister a couple of paces behind me.

I was getting careless about the scrunch of pine needles beneath my shoes, and suddenly the whispering, which had been faint, stopped altogether. I stopped too, and looked back for Fen, but there was no sign of her. I wanted to call out to her, but I didn't want anyone to hear me so I stayed silent. It shocked me to see the darkness behind as well as ahead of me. Behind was dim and shadowy, ahead was black and still. Even the flickering lights had stopped. Maybe they'd never been there at all. Perhaps I'd just imagined them.

"Come in Andy," came a voice out of the darkness, making me jump. I only hesitated for a moment, then moved in the direction of the voice. This was it, this was the meeting, and much as I shouldn't be there, there was no going back now.

Sack-cloth drapes had been hung between three or four trees, so it was impossible to see behind them. But then, as if on a time switch, the lights flickered again and the sack cloth grew blotchy with the eerie shadows of enlarged, mis-shapen heads. I had to go in, but I was scared.

One side of the sack cloth was slowly folded back to let me through, then dropped back into place behind me. I stared round. Sitting in a circle on the ground were fifteen or twenty people. They each held a candle or a torch. A boy of about sixteen sat on a tree trunk. His head was bent because he was writing in a notepad. Some of the people in the circle were watching him. The rest were watching me. The girl who had let me through the sack cloth was the one from the cinema. She didn't smile at me. None of them did. I spotted Sid sitting near to the boy on the tree trunk. From all around the circle, Ss glinted in the torch- and candlelight. Every single person wore one, girls and boys.

"So you found us," Sid said.

I didn't reply. There was no need.

"You told me you were already a member of the Strays, Andy," came another voice. I glanced round the circle till I spotted the speaker. It was the girl from the cinema, who had sat down.

"Yeah, I know. Sorry," I said simply, because there didn't seem any point in wasting time denying it.

"Who else is with you?" asked Sid.

"My friend Fen. She's just back there."

At that point, Twister, who had been standing perfectly still, good as gold, right behind me, came forward and barked at the assembled circle. Then as though joyfully spotting a great friend, he bounded over to Sid and started licking her face and barking at her, tail wagging. Sid reached out to stroke his head and he climbed into her lap. I glanced round the circle to see what effect this crazy dog was having on everybody else, but no one was particularly reacting. Sid herself was taking it all in her stride as though she'd known Twister for years.

"Does he know you?" I asked.

"Yeah," she said, as she continued to stroke the soppy animal. "I take him out for walks a lot. We're old buddies."

"We can't change the rules. You've still got to find an S before you can join," said a boy of about fifteen, suddenly sharpening up the atmosphere again.

"Yeah, that's fine, I'm going to."

"Right, shall we carry on with the meeting?" asked another boy, and realizing this was my cue to leave I went over and put Twister on the lead, then dragged him away from Sid. He really didn't want to go, but I was insistent. I just wanted to get away as fast as possible, because I felt a fool for having blundered into something uninvited.

It was a relief to meet up with Fen and another relief to come out of the trees into the bright morning light. Twister was bounding around happily, then he suddenly dropped something from his mouth and looked up at me, wagging his tail and barking.

"What's this?" Fen asked, picking up a black and red glove.

"It's Sid's. I recognize it from the other day," I replied.

"Hadn't we better take it back?" Fen asked, in a voice that hinted strongly that she really did not want to go back in there. I knew how she felt. No way was I going to interrupt that meeting a second time.

"We can give it back to her when we've joined the Strays properly," I said, and Fen was quick to agree, so we made our way back to the centre and I told her all about what I'd just seen.

"We ought to tell the others about the Strays and everything, now," said Fen. Then, when I didn't reply straight away, she added firmly, "Oughtn't we?"

"Yes, we will," I said, because I felt ready to tell the others now.

Chapter 8

Jaimini

Walking in the dales was wonderful. The sun came out and the sky turned blue. It was the best weather possible for the time of year. We played hide-and-seek in the woods, climbed hills and swung on the branches of trees. Then we stopped in a little sheltered place and ate muffins and chocolate. Everything was great, but the best fun of all was laying trails for each other.

We got back to the guest house just as night began to fall and we decided to see if we could get seats for the local pantomime. Jules was very doubtful about this.

"Don't get your hopes up," she said. "The pantomime always gets booked right up."

Sure enough there weren't any seats left and Helen was about to try and book for another night when the lady on the other end of the phone suddenly said, "Oh, wait a minute, I think we had a cancellation today. Let me see." She looked it up and came back to Helen with the news that there were four seats. Helen checked whether there might possibly be six or seven seats available for another night before we had to go back home, but there weren't, so she settled for the four.

"I don't mind not going," said Andy.

Then everybody said they didn't mind not going. Anyone listening would have thought that the idea was to try *not* to go to the pantomime! In the end we put all the names in a hat – well, a bowl actually – including Helen's. We also pretended to put Peta's in there, but we didn't really. Anyway, Peta didn't have a clue what we were talking about or what a pantomime was. Helen said it would be wasted on her because she'd be frightened by the villain, and then she'd fall asleep. She reckoned that it would be much better to wait until Peta was older before taking her to a pantomime.

The four names that came out of the hat were Fen, me, Luce and Andy, so that meant that Tash would be staying at the guest house with Leah and Helen. They said they didn't mind at all, but we all felt guilty and kept offering to give up our seats. Finally Helen stopped all that by saying that the rest of them were going to hire a video and eat pizza and banoffee pie, so then it seemed fairer. Jules had made the pizza and the banoffee pie because she was so grateful to everyone for being there to look after Twister and to house-sit while she went off with her boyfriend to have a nice time!

The pantomime was fantastic. It was Cinderella, but they'd completely altered the plot so that Cinderella didn't marry Prince Charming at all. She married one of the other guests at the ball because he owned two or three Rolls-Royces. There were six ugly sisters instead of two, and they did the most fantastic disco dance. The wicked stepmother, who was played by a young man, was the leading role and it was she who ended up with the prince. There were also a few parts for children of about our age. There were two boys and a girl who had to be really scruffy and poor. They had to come begging in the middle of the ball and in the end, all the guests became enchanted with them and pleaded with the king and queen to let them stay and entertain them. So they had a song-and-dance number to do, which they did very well. I secretly thought that Luce could have done it better, though, but then I'm prejudiced.

The only other children's part was for a very pretty dark girl who was supposed to be the daughter of Buttons. This was a much bigger part than the other children's. The girl had very few words to say but she was always at Buttons's side, and he obviously adored her. There was a little subplot where she got kidnapped about halfway through by this nasty gang of thugs, and Buttons went into a complete decline because he was so upset that his pride and joy had been taken away from him. Then at the very end of the ball she was returned, because the prince had pretended to have a whipround among the audience and he'd got enough money to pay the ransom. It was such a clever story. We all thought it was great.

During the interval Luce did a brilliant take-off of the wicked stepmother, and because we egged her on she kept it up all the time until we had to go back to our places. I went to the loo on my own at one point. The loos were on the ground floor and off from the foyer. As I passed the main doors I glanced outside and couldn't believe my eyes. There was Helen with *the man*, and they were holding hands and talking, gazing into each other's eyes. I couldn't wait to tell Luce what I'd seen.

"You're kidding," she breathed into the darkness of the auditorium when we were back in our places for the second half. "I wonder if she's told Tash and Leah?"

At the end of the panto we all went round to the stage

door. Fen and I got loads of autographs. Andy wasn't that bothered about autographs and Luce was only interested in one: the wicked stepmother's, who, of course, was really a man. It got quite embarrassing because when the actors and actresses had autographed Fen's and my programmes, they automatically passed on to Luce because she was standing right beside us. Luce being Luce, she didn't think there was anything wrong with saying "No, thank you," to the poor actors and actresses.

"Aren't you into autographs?" asked one actor, called Simon, who thought Luce's attitude quite interesting and amusing, fortunately.

"Oh yes, but I only want the wicked stepmother's," said Luce.

"D'you hear that, Rick? She only wants yours," Simon said, laughing at the man who was emerging from the stage door. "She recognizes a pro when she sees one."

The actor called Rick, who had played the part of the wicked stepmother went straight into his wicked stepmother voice with the strong Scottish accent that he'd used during the panto.

"Well, that must be because I *am* the only pro round here," he said loudly and jokingly to amuse his admiring fans and his fellow actors. Then blow me if Luce didn't answer him in exactly the same voice, with the accent absolutely spot on.

"I think you're mistaken, my good woman," she said. "*I'm* the only pro round here as it happens."

There was this stunned silence, then all the autograph hunters and the actors laughed and said how brilliant she was. Rick broke into a slow smile as he made his way towards us. He was not exactly handsome, but very tall and dark with strong features. I guessed he would be in his late twenties.

"That's a pretty big talent you've got there," he said softly to Luce, then he turned to me. "What about you, young lady? You an actress as well?" I shook my head. "Doesn't matter. With looks like yours, you don't need any talent."

I felt very flattered and didn't know what to say. Rick signed our three programmes (Andy was standing a little apart because she wasn't bothered about getting autographs) and asked Luce if she was local. When we explained that we were on holiday for a few days at West Lea Guest House, but that we actually lived miles away, he said it was a pity, because he could have done with someone like her to audition for a new play that they were going to be showing in March. As the rest of the autograph hunters drifted away, leaving just us and Rick with a couple of his friends, he even produced a script from his coat pocket and got Luce to read one of the speeches. Considering she'd never even seen it before, and she hadn't got much idea of what the play was all about, I thought she did it absolutely brilliantly. So did Rick.

"Well, Lucy Edmunson, I shall look out for your name in lights," he said as he went off with his friends into the night. "Good luck!"

"Thanks," replied Luce calmly, and the four of us got into the taxi that Helen had organized for us.

I felt really pathetic and little-girlish all of a sudden. Although I'd been flattered at the time to be called good-looking, now it seemed like a sort of consolation prize because I didn't have much else going for me. Luce was so lucky. She always got noticed no matter what she did. To make matters even worse, she was acting really maturely about it and somehow this made me feel more awful than ever, because it was like pouring salt into the wound. Not only was Luce very talented, she was also totally laid-back about it. Andy and Fen didn't seem bothered at all, but that was because they had their own talents. Fen was a great dancer and Andy was a brilliant athlete. I was just boring old me with no talent at all, but apparently it didn't matter because I was good-looking. Ha-ha.

We got back home at ten thirty and all sat round drinking hot chocolate while Luce entertained the others with a re-run of the entire pantomime. Tash and Leah were falling about laughing. Helen wasn't there (surprise, surprise!) because apparently when she'd put Peta to bed she'd said that she wouldn't mind going out for a breath of fresh air, and she'd asked the others if they were happy to watch the video on their own. When they'd assured her that was fine Helen had gone out, then she'd phoned about half an hour later to say that she'd come across someone that she'd met during the day and was having a drink in the pub with a few people, and that she'd be back at about eleven. Tash commented at that point that she felt as though she were the mother and Helen the naughty child staying out late. Anyway, that explained our sighting of Helen during the interval.

Tash

I had mixed feelings when I went to bed that night. Part of me wanted to hear the taps again to find out if they were going to spell out anything, but another part of me was scared because the tapping really unnerved me. Also, a part of me wanted to tell Fen about this mysterious thing that was going on in the night, then she could listen too, but another part of me was afraid that the tapping might stop altogether if Fen was listening.

It was very difficult to get Fen to fall asleep that night. She was in a chatty mood, mainly about the pantomime and how much Luce had impressed the actor Rick Somebody-or-other. But then, after she'd completely exhausted the subject of pantomimes and actors and Luce and everything to do with the evening, she still seemed to want to carry on talking. It was as though she had something important on her mind but didn't know how to start to tell me. I felt sorry for her in one way, but on the other hand I was dying for her to go to sleep so that I could wait for the tapping to start.

"Let's go to sleep, Fen. We'll talk in the morning, OK?"

"OK," she said, a bit reluctantly I thought.

We switched off the light because we both like sleeping in the dark, then I lay awake for ages concentrating on Fen's breathing to see whether or not she was asleep. I almost asked her, but I thought that if she wasn't asleep and I spoke to her, then she'd know that I wasn't asleep either, and she'd probably want to start talking again.

Eventually I knew she was definitely out because she said something in her sleep. Her voice sounded completely normal but she was talking nonsense. She said, "Are there two sinks or only one?"

"Where?" I asked carefully.

"In the bed," she answered.

"None," I told her, and she turned over with a big sigh.

It was probably a good five minutes after that that the tapping started. I'd been just drifting off to sleep, but when the first tap came, my eyes shot open and I woke right up, ready to count. There was the one loud tap, the same as last time, then this was followed by eight taps and then by nine and then by twenty. I couldn't believe it. This was exactly the same pattern as I'd counted the previous night. It was saying H-I-T again. So surely it must be a message of some sort. I had my torch all ready at my bedside and I had also written down on a piece of paper every letter in the alphabet and what number it was, up to twenty-six.

Every single nerve ending in my body was on red alert, waiting to work out the next letter and thus the next word. I waited and waited, but couldn't stay awake. The next thing I knew, Fen was at my side. My eyes flew open.

"What are you doing?"

"Switching off your torch," she whispered. "You must have fallen asleep with it on. It woke me up."

"Oh sorry," I mumbled.

"Why have you written down all the letters of the alphabet?" she then asked me as she shone the torch on to my paper, which had fallen from my hand on to the floor.

"Tell you tomorrow," I mumbled. She took the hint then and went back to bed. I had no intention of telling her the next day, but by then I might have thought of a good reason why I had the alphabet written out and numbered as my bedtime reading.

When I went back to sleep I dreamed that I was in a rounders match at school and the teacher kept on calling out to me to hit the ball. "Hit," she screamed loudly, but I kept on missing and running round, then rushing back to have another go. By the morning I was totally exhausted. The dream had left me with a funny feeling, but the main sensation I had was one of frustration because, once again, I hadn't got to the end of the message. Or maybe there wasn't an ending. Perhaps that was the complete message and I had to work out what on earth it could mean.

Leah

On the day that we were going to the Blue John mines, guess who felt ill? I don't know what was the matter with me: I just felt very tired and I had a temperature. Helen was so sorry for me and said that we could easily go to the Blue John mines another day, but I didn't want to feel ill and feel guilty at the same time, so I finished up by practically begging them all to go without me. Helen finally said that we'd do it all again when I was better.

Jules had offered to stay with me and Helen had taken her up on her kind offer, but I didn't want Jules to feel tied to the house all day.

"I'll be fine, honestly Helen. I don't need anyone to stay with me."

"I wouldn't be happy about leaving you on your own, Leah. Can you imagine if I had to tell your mum that you'd been abducted because I left you on your own for the day? Also, you're not well. You need someone to take care of you."

"But I feel as though I'm giving Jules an extra problem instead of making things better for her. She'll begin to wish she'd never agreed to us staying."

"No, I don't mind staying in at all, really," said Jules. But I could tell she was only being kind. I was sure she had planned to go out. I suddenly had a brainwave.

"If Luce's Auntie Alice is in, why don't I take her phone number, and she'll be there if I need anyone in a hurry. Like a sort of emergency number. That way, nobody will have to change their plans, but you won't have to worry about me, Helen."

"That's a good idea," said Helen. "I'll give her a call and check that she'll be in this morning."

"And I can be back around lunchtime anyway," said Jules, who seemed much happier about this new arrangement, so I'd obviously been right. She *did* want to go out somewhere.

Helen phoned Auntie Alice, and she said she hadn't planned to go out anywhere and that I mustn't hesitate for a second to contact her if I wanted anything at all, no matter how small. So after breakfast, off they all went. Funnily enough, it was Fen who seemed the most worried about me. She kept on saying, "Are you sure you're going to be all right, Lee?"

The empty house seemed very big and quiet when they'd all gone. I stayed in bed for about an hour and must have fallen asleep. When I woke up I felt much better. In fact I was very hungry and got up and made myself breakfast, then watched a bit of TV, but there was nothing much on.

"This is ridiculous," I said to myself as I paced about the house wondering what on earth to do. Then I had an idea that filled me with happiness. I would go into the town and see if I happened to bump into that boy. Maybe I'd walk past the cafe and see if I could see him. I didn't think I'd dare to go in if I did, but I could cross that bridge when I came to it.

Almost guiltily I got myself ready and left the guest house. I bought some magazines, then went into a couple of big stores and tried on two pairs of trousers and three tops. Next I looked all through the CDs at this huge shop called Music Now. As I was flicking through, I was keeping an eye on the door and also the rest of the store, praying that *he* would come in. After that I looked at the messages inside about a hundred birthday cards in a card shop. Then, finally, I took my courage in both hands and made for the cafe.

At first I passed it quite quickly and only glanced in fleetingly, but then when I got to the other side, I thought that was silly because I hadn't been able to see a thing. So then I crossed the road and stood right opposite the cafe pretending that I was meeting someone there. This meant that I could keep taking furtive glances through the window, and although I was quite a distance away, I could see more like this than I had been able to when I'd rushed past at a hundred miles per hour.

On my third glance, my heart stoped beating because I felt sure that he *was* in there. The person that I thought was him was sitting sideways to the window and chatting with two other boys. I tried to see if Emma was anywhere around, but it was very difficult to tell. I felt nervous and quite guilty, standing there. I knew there was no chance of my seeing the others because they'd gone off on a special coach to the Blue John mines, but I'd decided that if, by any awful coincidence, I ran into Jules I would just say that I had started to feel better after everyone had gone, and I felt so bored that I'd decided to go out and buy a magazine or two to read. That was true, of course, but it would be very difficult to explain what I was doing standing staring in at a cafe window from across the road.

I was just wondering whether to go back to the guest house when the boy looked out and saw me. I immediately looked the other way because I didn't want him to think I'd been staring, and then I took a quick look at my watch, to make it look as though I was waiting for someone. When I next glanced up it was to see him coming out of the cafe towards me. Our eyes met and he gave me the most beautiful smile so I smiled back, feeling a rush of happiness. This day was turning out to be quite good after all! Unfortunately I had spoken too soon because the very next second Luce's Auntie Alice was at my side.

"Hello, my duck, I thought it was you. What are you doing? I thought you were ill?"

"I'm . . . I'm . . . I'm better." The boy had stopped when he'd seen me being approached by Auntie Alice. He was kind of hovering, unsure what to do, and I felt so sorry for him. Much as I've got nothing at all against poor old Auntie Alice, at that moment in time I did not want her within a ten-mile radius of me. I had to get rid of her. And quickly. "The others went off, and I suddenly thought I'd come into town for a while."

"So what are you doing standing here, dear? Not waiting for a taxi, I hope."

"No, I was just, you know, standing here." Oh, what a stupid answer. What *was* I burbling on about?

"You'll catch your death standing around like this, love. Come on, I'll take you back. My car's only just around the corner and it gets warm as toast in there in no time at all."

She was ushering me along, and all I could do was give the boy the most apologetic, helpless smile I could, and hope that he'd understand that this was definitely not my choice. He looked as fed up as I felt as he turned and went back into the cafe. The journey back to the guest house in Auntie Alice's hot little car was one of the most depressing of my life. I'd been so near to talking to that boy, but once again fate had been against me. The only thing that lifted my spirits was that the sky was filling up with big soft snowflakes, bundling and bursting all over the world below. It's very difficult to stay depressed when you see snow for the first time after a long, long wait. I just kept staring up at it and hoping and hoping that it would continue for ages.

Chapter 9

Leah

Auntie Alice stayed for a cup of tea and a chat. It was one of the most one-sided chats in history, I should think, because Auntie Alice could chat the hind legs off a donkey. She told me about a million snow-related stories and interspersed them with "I can't think where Jules has got to" and "Goodness knows where that girl is" and "I'm going to have to go in a minute. Will you be all right?" and other such phrases. I assured her I'd be fine and eventually she *did* go and the silence was lovely. It wasn't that I didn't appreciate Auntie Alice, just that I wanted the time to daydream about the boy. I flipped through my magazines, but I wasn't really concentrating on them. Then I suddenly remembered Twister. Where was that dog? Surely Jules hadn't taken him with her? But she must have done because there had been no sign of him anywhere in the house and I hadn't heard any barking at all. He would have barked when Auntie Alice and I had come in together, surely?

Just as I was having this thought someone knocked at the door. Oh good, that must be Jules. But had she forgotten her key? I leaped up to answer the door and got quite a shock to see not Jules but three people I didn't recognize at

111

all. The boy looked about sixteen and the two girls probably about the same age. They were all chewing gum and they just stood there with their heads on one side, kind of surveying me as though I was an interesting species of monkey behind bars that couldn't avoid their curious stares.

One of the girls, whose hair was bright crimson, put her hand against the wall just outside the front door and leaned on it casually as though she was waiting for something, and was prepared to wait all day. She was wearing two nose rings and another ring in her eyebrow. She had tons of eye make-up on, but her face looked a bit damp because of the snow, and some of the black had smudged underneath her eyes. The other girl was very thin and white-faced. She was wearing a leather skirt and a thin T-shirt underneath a big woolly sort of cardigan coat. The boy wore jeans and a leather jacket. That was all I took in, apart from their cold stares, which really unnerved me.

"Jules isn't here," I stammered, knowing that it was a stupid thing to say but having to say something because the silence was embarrassing and frightening.

"Good. We ain't looking for Jules. We're looking for Leah." It was the girl with the crimson hair talking. She pronounced the first part of my name Lee, but the second part like the sound of the O in the word on. I suddenly felt absolutely terrified and quickly tried to slam the door shut, but the boy's reactions were faster than mine. He wedged his foot against the door so I couldn't shut it, and all three of them laughed, only it wasn't a proper laugh.

"Ain't yer going to ask us in then, Leah?" said the thin girl, grinning at me.

I didn't know what to say so I didn't say anything, but my mind was working at a rate of knots. I wondered whether

I ought to try and rush past them and just keep running and running in the hope that I might meet someone before they caught me up. But I couldn't do that. They might burgle the house. Then I wondered whether to let them in then try to slip away to phone the police.

"Leah's not here," I finally said.

That made them fall about laughing and I tried again to shut the door, but the boy slammed his foot back into position too quickly. The next thing I knew they were all in the house and I was standing in the middle of the sitting room. The boy shut the front door and leaned against it with his arms folded, watching me with an amused expression on his face. The girls went upstairs as though they lived here. For two or three minutes there was silence in the sitting room because neither the boy nor I spoke a single word. We could both hear the muffled voices of the girls upstairs and their footsteps as they went from room to room.

"The owners will be back any time," I said to the boy, trying to sound cool and unbothered.

"No they won't. The owners ain't here. They're on 'oliday."

"Yes, but I mean the people who are house-sitting for them."

"Yeah? Well, I think we'll take the risk," he grinned. "Emma don't like you, you know."

"Doesn't she?"

"Nah. She don't like dobbers with big gobs, see? So we said we'd come and get a bit even, and she said to make sure to go back and tell 'er all about the look on your face, cos she reckons you're a bit too fond of yourself. She doesn't miss much, Emma doesn't, so you needn't think you can get your claws into her Jake, you know. She saw the way you were looking at him."

"But I didn't—" I started to say.

"And yer talk posh, an' all, like yer friend with the lip."

At that point the two girls appeared, and I trembled to think what might happen next. I didn't think I'd ever felt so frightened in my life.

"This is nice, Shal," said the one with red hair as she picked up the TV remote control.

"Yeah, we need one of them," said the thin girl.

"It'll only work on this telly," I said, feeling the hairs on my arms standing on end.

"Nah, it works on any telly," said the girl with the red hair, laughing like a hyena.

Then I noticed what the other girl wore on her wrist. It was Fen's watch. "We don't think much of your friends' taste in clothes and things, 'cept for this watch. It's really cute, isn't it? We like this one, don't we, Fay?" She was twisting her arm this way and that to show off the watch. I felt sick with worry. "We was thinking about where you keep yer money."

Suddenly I heard the most welcome sound I thought I'd ever heard. It was a very low growl. Come on Twister, come in here, I prayed. My prayer was answered. I didn't know where on earth he'd been all morning, but right now he was at the door, teeth bared, the growl now stronger and more menacing.

"He wants you to put down the watch and the TV control. He's really dangerous, I'm warning you. He'll bite you."

I was trying to sound as though I was worried about what Twister might do because he really *was* a ferocious dog. Really and truly I knew that Twister had never bitten anyone in his life. He just snapped and growled and pretended to be fierce. The two girls weren't sure if I was lying or not. The boy looked scared, though.

"Come on, we've had our fun. Let's get going," he said.

"She's kidding. This old thing wouldn't hurt a flea," said the girl called Fay.

"I'm not kidding, honestly. Twister once ripped someone's arm off," I said in the most look-I'm-serious-about-this voice I could muster.

"Oh yeah? So why wasn't he put down then? She's trying to fool us. Can't you see, Bricko?"

Then Twister leaped at the boy and snapped at him, narrowly missing his leg.

"Right, that's it. I'm off!" said Bricko. "Come on you two. Let's get out of here. Drop the things and get a move on."

"Don't drop the things. He can't be *that* clever. He doesn't know we've nicked a watch, for God's sake."

Just as though Twister could understand every word that was being spoken, he launched himself at the girl wearing Fen's watch and nearly knocked her down.

"He *does* know, an' all," said the thin girl as she and the other one rushed out behind the boy, slamming the door shut behind them. I immediately locked and bolted it, then flopped back on to the settee because my legs had turned to jelly. Twister came and lay at my feet.

"So Jules is wrong about you, isn't she?" I whispered as I patted and cuddled Twister and told him what a brilliant boy he was. He licked my hand and twisted round and round and round. I felt so fond of him. He'd been a wonderful guard dog.

At that moment, in walked Jules.

"Hi, Leah, sorry I'm later than I thought. Isn't the snow incredible? It's going to be totally white by this evening." She stopped and stared. "Goodness me. I don't believe it. I thought Twister growled at you the other night. He doesn't usually change his mind about people, you know. Maybe it's because he senses that you're not well. How are you, by the way? Sorry, I should have asked you that straight away."

"I'm feeling better thanks. I mean, I feel completely recovered," I said, hoping that my white-faced, big-eyed look wasn't too much of a giveaway.

"Really? You don't look it. You're still looking very peaky and pale."

"No, no, I'm fine, honestly."

Jules had been looking round the room as she'd been talking. "Where *is* that remote control? I want to catch the weather."

"Oh, er, I'm not sure." My heart hammered. How was I going to get out of this one? I'd had no time to think about anything. There was no way I could tell her about those three friends of Emma's turning up. If I did, I'd have to explain why, and that would only go to show how deceitful I'd been. Also, Jules might get the wrong idea about what had happened in the cafe.

"Oh, here it is. What's it doing down here?" She picked it up from beside the front door where one of the girls must have dropped it. I couldn't help the huge sigh of relief that escaped. As soon as Jules sat down in front of the television, I had a subtle look near the front door, praying that Fen's watch might be there too. No such luck. I couldn't understand why Fen hadn't been wearing her watch, but it must have been either that she'd forgotten it, or that she'd thought it might get damaged so she'd decided to keep it safe in her room. The horrible thought suddenly struck me that Shal and Fay might have helped themselves to other things that I didn't know about. I left Jules with the weather report and went upstairs to check the bedrooms. As far as I could see nothing else had been taken, but I didn't know if anyone had left any money lying around.

Everything had gone so horribly wrong for me now. I was left with the problem of how to tell Fen that her watch had got stolen. The more I thought about it, the more I decided there was no way I could. I'd have to pretend that the events of the afternoon had never happened and that I was as shocked and baffled as everyone else about the missing watch. My pulse beat faster just thinking about it. How I wished I could rewind this whole holiday back to the very beginning and start all over again.

Fen

We had the most fantastic day at the caves and in the little town looking round all the souvenir shops. Just about the whole town was made up of shops and cafes. Luce and Jaimini bought earrings and rings and a pendant each. I didn't buy anything for myself, but I bought a ring for Mum, a necklace for Rachel and a bracelet for Emmy. We all had a field day. Tash and her mum bought a pendant necklace, which they agreed to share. Andy bought a ring for Leah, which I thought was really sweet of her, and also a chain to wear round her neck for herself. I bet I knew what that was for. We phoned Leah during the morning but there was no reply. She must have been asleep. We phoned again in the afternoon and Jules answered. She said that Leah was miles better. We didn't want to make her too envious of us for our brilliant day out but I knew we were all dying to tell her about the caves, which were fantastic.

The Blue John stone glinting in the seams of the caves deep, deep underground was an incredible sight. The best cave was the one where the guide had to steer the boat through the narrow passages with his feet on the roof. There were lots of lights all the way along the passages but they were so very narrow and low, in fact, only just wide enough for the boat, and I felt quite claustrophobic. Helen, Tash and Luce wouldn't go into that cave because they were worried about feeling closed in. But Andy, Jaimes and I went, and I'm really glad we did. The cafe that we had lunch in was absolutely sweet. There were so many cafes to choose from and ours was a tiny one with only three tables altogether. I had quiche, chips and salad. It was the best quiche I'd ever tasted.

We couldn't believe it when the snow started because there was no warning or build-up at all. It just came down suddenly and dramatically in great big lumps from the sky. The five of us let out a big cheer because we'd all been dying for it to snow. Peta thought it was magic, but Helen groaned and said that snow was very nice to look at, but not so wonderful to drive in. It was true. The coach had to go more slowly on the way back because the roads were slippery.

"Hi, Lee. How are you?" we all cried as we tumbled into the sitting room. It was dark and it felt lovely and cosy in the guest house. Jules had lit a fire. We'd bought doughnuts for tea. They tasted almost as nice as my quiche. I decided to have a bath, so I went upstairs.

For some reason or other I couldn't find my watch anywhere. I'd deliberately not taken it with me because I didn't want to scratch it or damage it in the caves. I got it for Christmas from Mum and Dad and I absolutely love it because it's a designer watch and I've never owned anything like it before.

"Has anyone seen my watch?" I asked, going into the sitting room and cutting right through the middle of a conversation that they were all having.

"When did you last see it?" asked Helen, while the others all looked at me blankly.

"Before we went. I'm pretty certain I left it on the dressing chest. I deliberately didn't take it in case I scratched it or something."

"Well, then, it must still be there," said Helen. "Have you checked behind the chest?"

I hadn't, so I went back up and searched Tash's and my bedroom thoroughly. The watch was nowhere. While I was searching I came across the crumpled piece of paper that Tash had been looking at the previous night. Why had she written out the alphabet and numbered each letter, then taken the paper and a torch to bed with her? It was a weird thing to do, and seemed like some kind of secret from me. She'd said she would explain it today, but she hadn't said a word.

Then there was Leah. She was behaving rather oddly. She seemed kind of upset. Even now, although she was saying she felt completely better, she didn't really look it. As if all that wasn't bad enough, there was also Jaimini and Luce. They'd got some kind of a secret, I was sure. I'd seen them whispering together at the panto and at various other times. It crossed my mind that everybody might be in on everybody else's secrets and I was the only one who was being kept in the dark. Maybe they were all sitting downstairs, knowing precisely what had happened to my watch, but nobody was telling me because I was the outsider. To be fair, though, Andy and I had got a secret, too. We were going to tell the others, though. In fact, it was supposed to have been during the day today, but with Leah being ill we'd decided to put it off till she was better. I sat down on the bed then flopped back and put my hands behind my head, linking my fingers and staring at the ceiling, trying to weigh things up. This was how Tash found me when she came up a few minutes later.

"I thought you were having a bath. Did you find your watch? Are you all right, Fen?"

"Not really."

"What's the matter?" asked Tash, sitting down on the bed and giving me her most anxious look.

"I don't know where my watch is."

"Well, it *must* be somewhere. I'll help you look for it, shall I?"

"And I don't understand why everybody's got secrets." There, I'd said it. Tash looked puzzled.

"Secrets? I thought you and Andy had got a secret, actually."

"Well, it's not exactly a secret, just something that we haven't got round to saying yet. But we will, honestly, tonight."

"So who else has got a secret?" Tash asked.

"I thought *you* had. Couldn't you just let me into the reason for reading the alphabet by torchlight at nighttime, Tash?"

"OK," she agreed, surprisingly easily, and then we sat on the bed together and I heard all about the tapping noises that Tash had been hearing, and how they spelt out the word "hit". She said that they didn't quite sound the same as the ones she'd heard on the first day, but she couldn't pinpoint what the difference was. She hadn't told anyone else, because she had the feeling that the taps were meant personally for her and she was dying to hear what the next word was. Once she'd told me all this, and seen how much I shared her excitement, Tash seemed really happy.

"We can listen together tonight," she said. "I must admit I was beginning to get slightly spooked by the whole thing. It'll be good having someone else to listen. After all, it's ridiculous to think that a ghost could possibly know whether or not you're asleep. I mean, you might have been lying there with your eyes closed, but your ears really alert."

After this conversation we had another look for my watch, and right in the middle, I glanced up to see Leah standing in the doorway. Her face was white and her eyes were big and afraid.

"Something terrible happened today," she said, in scarcely more than a whisper.

"Whatever's the matter Lee?" asked Tash, jumping up from behind the bed.

"I came to see Fen. I've got something to tell you, but I'll tell you both."

"Is it something to do with my watch?" Fen asked. Then, when Leah didn't reply, just stared at her with big tearful eyes, she said, "You haven't broken my watch, have you Lee?"

"Worse than that."

"What?"

"Two girls and a boy forced their way in this afternoon. They were all about sixteen and they were really horrible to me and then they stole your watch, Fen."

Leah had told us this through her tears. Tash and I stared

at each other, speechless. Poor Leah. She'd been in terrible danger and scared out of her wits. It was an unbelievable thing she was telling us.

"Why didn't you tell anyone, Lee?"

"Because it's all my fault."

"But how can it be your fault? You can't help it if someone breaks in."

"Because I was the one who Emma didn't like. You see, there was this boy in the cafe, and I kept looking at him, and Andy thinks that maybe Emma had her eye on him, or worse, maybe he was actually her boyfriend or something, because she looked daggers at me when she realized that the boy had seen me looking at him. The people who broke in were Emma's friends. She'd sent them on purpose to—"

"To what, Lee?" asked Tash.

"To frighten me. You know."

"Oh, Lee, that's terrible. We've got to tell Andy and the others. But you mustn't blame yourself. That's ridiculous," I said, feeling pretty scared just listening to what had happened. It was definitely time to have a meeting and tell the others about the Strays.

So a few minutes later, while Helen was giving Peta a bath and Jules was watching telly, the six of us had a big meeting. We all sat round on the floor in our room and Leah told the story about her terrible afternoon. Jaimini, Andy and Luce were as outraged as Tash and I had been, and I could see Andy's mind working away all the time Leah was talking. Then it was her turn. And as she talked the others hung on to her every word, especially the bit about the meeting that she'd kind of blundered into. Luce was absolutely loving the whole story and was determined that we should go out to Bracken Valley right there and then, in search of Ss. When we pointed out that it was actually rather dark for that, she agreed to put it off till the following morning. But the meeting wasn't over yet, because Tash told the others about the taps she'd been hearing, too. Talk about spilling secrets. What a day this was turning out to be!

Chapter 10

Luce

It was certainly a great evening for finding things out, because after the story of the mysterious Strays, we all got to hear the "Tash and the mysterious taps" story. Much as I sympathized with Leah, and although I'd been as gripped as everyone else by the awful tale she had to tell, I had great faith in Andy's ability to sort it all out, and this tapping thing was even more interesting. I wanted to hear it. We all did.

So I came up with a great plan of action. I reckoned that we could all go out for a nice walk in the snow, maybe throw a few snowballs on the way, then buy some goodies for a midnight feast. The feast would, of course, take place in Tash and Fen's room and then we could all be on the alert for "things that go bump in the night". The waitress at the cafe had used that phrase, and now we were beginning to see what she meant.

Andy was the only one of us who wasn't totally bowled over by my wonderful plan, but then Andy had her mind on other things. I forgave her for her secrecy about the Strays, because Jaimini and I were still hanging on to our secret about Helen and *the man*. The Strays did sound a bit weird, though. I had this mental picture of a pack of very scruffy dogs that nobody wanted, holding meetings in secret places, with Andy sitting in the middle of them. But that's just me. I know I'm crazy. I get told it often enough.

The snow was fantastic. Why didn't we get swirly flakes that weighed about half a kilo each where we lived? I did a wild dance to show my appreciation of this wonderful snow, and the others fell about laughing because I hadn't realized, as I was cavorting about, that I'd attracted a little group of onlookers who were staring at me as though I'd completely lost my marbles. The first I knew about my exclusive audience was when they burst into applause. It didn't bother me, I just bowed and thanked them for their appreciation.

"Lucy Edmunson!" said a voice from the snowy dark. I stopped and stared. It was Rick from the pantomime. "You really are too good to be true," he went on. This time I didn't go showing off with a broad Scottish accent and a clever line, I just thanked him in a very refined and grown-up manner, then we parted. I felt very happy, though. Sometimes I was glad to be me, funny though that must seem.

We went to a sweet shop then to a cake shop where we stocked up with the best goodies we could find for the least possible money. As we walked along Andy invented challenges, such as who could hit a certain post with a snowball, and things like that. We all felt so happy at that moment, full of wintery, snowy, Cafe Club happiness. The only thing that was spoiling our lovely holiday was the thought of what had happened to poor Leah. She'd told us countless times that she wished she could click her fingers and get Fen's watch back. She still felt as though it was her fault, even though Fen kept on telling her not to worry, and Andy kept on telling her that she'd sort it out. Goodness knows how Andy intended getting the watch back. It would be rather like recovering a needle from the bottom of the sea. Still, Andy did have a knack of achieving the impossible.

At midnight my alarm went off and Jaimes and I crept along the passage into Tash and Fen's room. I nearly had a heart attack when we bumped into someone on the way, but it was only Andy and Leah.

"Why didn't you say anything?" I demanded of Andy.

"Because I couldn't see you any more than you could see me," Andy replied in a whisper. Tash and Fen hadn't been to sleep at all. They'd set out all the food and drink, and we all sank into our quilts on the carpet.

"Have you heard anything yet?" I asked.

"Not a thing," replied Tash. "I hope it doesn't turn out to be a waste of time."

"Ssh! Better keep our voices down. We don't want Helen or Peta waking up," said Fen. She did have a point. They were in the room right next door, after all.

So for the next two minutes we were silent, which, believe me, was very boring. What was also quite a challenge for me was keeping my hands off all that lovely food. I was the one who finally suggested that we just enjoy our feast and have a nice time (not easy when you've got to whisper!), and forget all about ghosts and ghouls. Then if any tapping did start, we'd stop our chatter and pay attention.

Everybody agreed with my plan so we tucked in greedily, then took turns to tell jokes. It was when we were on the second round of jokes and it was my turn that we all jumped halfway to the ceiling as one very clear, loud knock sounded. There was a great flurry of paper as we each consulted our copies of the numbered alphabet, then fell silent, wide-eyed.

"Eight," we mouthed to each other, at the end of the next batch of knocks.

"Nine," we mouthed again, after another series.

"It'll be twenty. It always is," I whispered. But I was wrong because there weren't any more taps at all.

We waited and waited, eyes darting everywhere, but there was nothing. I couldn't believe that the tapping had stopped already.

"Let's imagine that the T is there, too," said Jaimini. "Hit what? Everybody think."

"Hit the roof?" I suggested. "Something Mum does regularly," I added, but nobody laughed.

"Well, that's not a message," said Fen.

"You think of something better then," I said rather indignantly, because no one else was coming up with anything better. In fact, I turned out to be the only one with any ideas. "Hit lucky?"

"No," said Tash, shaking her head and not even bothering to look up.

"Hit me with your rhythm stick?" No answer, just a load of frowning faces staring at the floor. "Hit the nail on the head?" I was really pleased with that one, but again no one seemed very impressed. I began to wonder why I was working so hard to come out with all these gems when no one could even show an atom's-worth of interest. "Hit rock bottom?"

"Luce, they're all expressions, not messages," said Leah gently.

"Well, I don't know why you're all trying to think of things that start with 'hit' anyway," I said.

"Maybe the message means, 'Hit on the head the idea that this knocking is from another world, because it's actually coming from next door,'" suggested Andy, without altering her expression.

"So you're saying that it's pure coincidence that the knocks have spelled a definite word?" I asked her, thinking what a killjoy she was being.

"I reckon the knocking was coming from that wall there," Andy said. "So who sleeps there?"

"Peta," Tash replied.

"Exactly," said Andy. "And I reckon Peta's kicking the wall in her sleep."

"But wouldn't Helen have heard her?" Fen said.

Andy shrugged. "Maybe she's a deep sleeper."

"We've got to see," I squeaked, I was so excited. "Shall I go next door and watch?"

"Let's all go," Leah suggested. So we tiptoed down the passage and Tash very gently opened the door to Helen and Peta's room. They were both sound asleep. Peta's bedclothes were on the floor. Peta had her thumb in her mouth and was lying on her back, but as we watched she began to move restlessly from side to side. Each time she moved to the left the bed head banged on the wall.

"I'll listen from our room," said Fen, creeping off. "Count how many next time," she added. So we did. There were eight.

"She's cold," Tash whispered to the rest of us. "That's why she's moving about like that. She knows there's something not quite right, but she's too fast asleep to be able to do anything about it."

With that she got the quilt and laid it gently back over Peta, who curled up like a happy little hedgehog. Then we all crept back to Fen, who said there had definitely been eight knocks, but they hadn't sounded the same. "Mystery solved," said

Fen, but for some reason I didn't feel as though the mystery was solved. There seemed to be a piece of the jigsaw missing, but I couldn't for the life of me think what it was.

Leah

Andy and I got a shock when we pulled back the curtains to see a white world. There was a watery sun making the snow glisten and sparkle. We just stared through the window for ages because it was such an incredible sight.

"Wait till Luce sees this lot," Andy said, after at least a minute of silent staring.

As if on cue, in burst Luce with Jaimini and the others. The snowploughs had been out and the road had been cleared and gritted, leaving greyish remains, but the pavements and gardens had coat after coat of deep, thick, white snow. In no time at all we were dressed and out in the guest house's back garden building a snowman.

Peta came to join us after a little while. I didn't think I'd ever seen her quite so involved with anything. At first she had been so excited that she'd kept on falling over. The snow was too deep for her to stand in without it going into the tops of her wellies, so we'd cleared narrow passages for her to run along. She loved having her own personal road and spent ages weaving round us on her little track, singing and skipping. Then she'd stood perfectly still and watched what we were doing with a look of total fascination on her face. When finally she'd sussed what a snowman was, she decided to make her own.

"Is she behaving herself?" Helen called out of the kitchen window.

"She's no trouble at all," we all assured her, then Tash asked Helen if we could go to Bracken Valley, and Helen said she thought that was a great idea. Jules got the map out and we sat round one of the tables in the breakfast room, studying it.

"It's two miles from here, so why don't you take my car, Helen?" Jules suggested. "And take the two sledges. I'm afraid I haven't got any others, but those huge plastic bags make excellent sledges, and we've got a few of those round here."

We all cheered and went to sort out the plastic bags and the sledges and load them in the car. Next we packed up loads of provisions, including flasks of hot chocolate and bacon rolls. At last we were all ready to go.

It was decided that Helen and Peta would go by car with Jaimini, Luce, Tash and Twister, while Andy, Fen and I, "the crazy exercise freaks" as Luce described us, would walk the two miles to Bracken Valley. I was looking forward to the walk because I love the snow. It has such a magical atmosphere and it gives me a lovely warm feeling. But the main reason for walking was because it increased my chances of coming across *the* boy.

We walkers set off first and after about twenty minutes we were tooted by Helen, who passed us in Jules's car, and waved at vigorously by Luce out of the rear window.

"Do you think she's trying to see how many waves she can fit in before we're out of sight?" Andy asked, shaking her head at Luce's total madness. Twister barked and did a quick turn, then walked on faithfully. We broke into a jog after that, and I was quite impressed with myself for managing to keep up with the others for a full four minutes, but then gradually my legs got heavier and I felt so puffed out that I had to go back to walking. The others took pity on me and we all walked the rest of the way, apart from the very last bit, which we ran with great excitement, having spotted Helen's car.

A great scream suddenly pierced the snowy, calm, deserted world and after our initial shock we realized that this was Luce having the best kind of fun. She had just gone careering down a very steep slope on a plastic bag, and landed in a heap at the bottom. There was no one else in sight and it really felt as though we'd arrived in the most glorious winter wonderland. Bracken Valley was a vast dip, sunk into an area of very high ground. Within this dip there were little separate hills and valleys carved out, and it was down one of these little hills that Luce had just pelted.

"Doesn't it hurt your bottom?" I asked with my usual anxiety.

"No, it's such thickly padded snow, and I've got a thickly padded bottom too," she replied brightly. "They must have had twice as much snow up here as they've had in the town."

Twister launched himself off the hill with wild abandon and half ran, half rolled all the way down to the bottom, which raised a laugh. Then I took courage, along with everyone else, and we all had a go at sledging down the same hill, because it was the best one. Helen and Peta went down a much less steep hill some distance away, and we could hear Peta's excited laughter tinkling across the valley. There were now other voices echoing round the valley, too. Loads of people must have decided to come out and have fun, just like us. Twister spent his time dashing from Peta and Helen to us. Andy and Fen then went trudging off with one of the proper sledges to climb the biggest hill we could see, then they lay on their stomachs, one on top of the other (Andy on top because she's the lightest) and sledged all the way down. Neither of them screamed even though we saw them both tumble off quite near the bottom and roll over two or three times.

"Are you OK?" I yelled out at the top of my voice, and they both jumped up and yelled back that it was fantastic, so then we all decided to try it out. Helen and Peta had found a little sheltered place where Peta was happily involved with making another embryonic snowman and Helen was standing watching the world go by.

"Are you all right, Mum?" Tash called out.

"Perfect," came the answer, and it was true that Helen did look perfectly happy. "Take this sledge," she added. "We don't need it at the moment."

So with two sledges and two plastic bags we went up and down in different combinations. The funniest had to be Twister and Luce on the same sledge. After a bit I found that I was completely relaxed, not even worrying when the sledges swerved or jolted. Another very funny moment was when Luce impulsively decided to take off down the opposite side of the hill. There were several bales of hay wrapped up tightly in plastic, with thick cord around them, dotted around this side of the hill, which was why we'd decided not to risk sledging here. But Luce being Luce sailed off on her own without telling anyone. The first we knew about it was when this big scream rose into the air. Andy and I had just climbed to the top of the hill ready for our next go when we looked over the other side and saw that Luce had hit a bale, bringing her sledge to an abrupt halt, while she herself had been catapulted up into the air and was spreadeagled on top of the bale.

"Oh great!" came her sarcastic voice from below. Andy and I beckoned to Tash and Fen and Jaimini to hurry up to the top, which they did. And there the five of us stood, laughing hysterically at the sight of Luce scrambling down from the hay bale and pretending she'd purposely pulled that little stunt.

"You should try it! It's quite difficult steering your sledge so you hit the bale at exactly the right angle," she called out enthusiastically, but that only made us laugh all the more because we knew she'd had no intention of hitting the bale in the first place.

"What about looking for Ss?" Fen suddenly said, but at that precise moment we heard the sound of Peta crying. After a couple of minutes when it didn't stop, we all went zooming down to find out what the matter was. When we got to the little sheltered spot we found Helen removing two totally soggy socks from Peta's right foot and trying to dry her off with some kitchen roll from the picnic basket.

"She put her foot down a hole full of water," Helen explained. "The trouble is, you can't tell what's a hole and what isn't. There's a thin layer of ice then it's covered with snow so it looks like solid ground, but underneath it's full of water where the ice has melted."

Helen transferred one of Peta's socks from her left foot to her right one, then we all tried to cheer up Peta by talking about Luce and her antics.

"Do you mind, you lot!" Luce said indignantly. "I think there's rather a lot of laughing being done at my expense here."

"We wouldn't have half as much fun if you weren't around, Luce," Jaimini assured her best friend, as Helen dished out bacon rolls from the picnic basket and poured out hot chocolate. Peta kept on crying, off and on, all the way through our picnic, and Helen said that she thought she'd better take her back home because she was cold and tired. It was only lunchtime and the rest of us were nowhere near ready to go back yet. We were still boiling hot from all the sledging, and now our insides were warm as well from the hot chocolate and the food.

"When you're ready to come home, give me a ring from that phone box just near to where I parked the car," Helen suggested before she went off with a still-whingeing Peta and the picnic basket. Twister stayed with us because he was no trouble and he was certainly enjoying himself. He'd had a whole bacon roll and a few other little titbits, too. As we waved Helen and Peta off, a group of boys turned up and started sledging where we'd just been.

"How dare they sledge on our hill," Luce said indignantly.

"It's a free world, Luce," Jaimes told her.

"Not this bit. This bit's our private sledging territory," Luce replied.

"Wouldn't it be good if it were," Fen said, and that got us exchanging stories about what kind of a place we'd want to own privately if we could choose anywhere in the world. My place was in my imagination. It didn't exist, but the others reckoned it would be possible to create it. It was like Disneyland without any of the rides or the characters, just the atmosphere, with the lights and the music and the huge archways, but it was set on a beach by the sea, surrounded by palm trees.

"How can you be thinking about beaches and palm trees when we're in the middle of winter?" Fen asked me. It was easy. I could transport myself anywhere in my imagination.

After a bit we got sick of dragging the sledges and the

bags around, so we hid them under a big crevice and went off searching for Ss.

"This is a totally impossible task!" Luce announced, hands on hips. "I mean, look at it. We'd need six shovels and three days digging to even stand half a chance."

"Luce's right," said Jaimini.

"Thank you, Jaimes. At least that's one more person who's seeing reason."

"I've just got a feeling that it's not entirely impossible," said Andy. "Let's think about it carefully. I mean, if you were going to hide something so small in a great big valley like this, where would you put it? And remember, Sid said there were loads of them hidden all over the place, so surely we should be able to find at least one," she went on.

"Let's not be too ambitious," I suggested. "Let's just see if we can find one."

"But that means that only one person will be able to join," said Andy.

"Well, I don't mind not joining," I said. "It doesn't sound like my kind of thing, really."

Then, one by one, the others all agreed. Even Fen.

"It's going to be boring for all you lot then," Andy said, looking worried.

"No, it's not. We'll all just look for one. I'm quite sure there isn't a single Stray who imagined even for a moment that we'd be able to find six Ss in these snowy conditions."

So it was settled. The aim was to find just one. And I bet I knew who would be the one to find it.

Chapter 11

Andy

I'd had a feeling about finding the S ever since Sid first mentioned it, and even when the snow seemed to be smothering the last chance of finding anything, let alone an S, I still didn't lose my positive feeling. The others appointed me as a kind of leader of the search without anyone actually saying anything, so I set the pace, deliberately not going too fast because I didn't want anyone to get fed up and feel like chucking it in. Twister kept rushing off and at first we were worried, but when we realized that he always came back, we managed to relax and let him do as he pleased. The other thing that was driving me to find an S was the fact that I knew I'd feel such a great sense of failure if I didn't. As we walked, Leah kept on turning round to look at the route we'd taken.

"It's because I've got no sense of direction," she explained. "I have to keep getting a mental picture of what it looks like for when we're coming back."

"Don't worry, I'm following the route carefully on the map," I told her, but actually I was sounding more confident than I was feeling because it wasn't easy with all the snow around. I got my orienteering badge last year, but this was

136

the first test in real live conditions. Tash is excellent at following maps so she was striding out in front with me and we stopped every so often to see where we were. The others kept their eyes on the ground all the time, and Luce muttered more or less continuously that it was a waste of time because an S wasn't going to appear suddenly, glinting conveniently on top of the snow.

For some reason I'd never thought of finding an S on the ground. I thought it would be more likely to be hanging on something. Every time we came to a bit of landscape that looked at all unusual I insisted on thoroughly examining every overhanging hillock or rock. All the while I could feel the others losing interest, until in the end I was the only one searching while the rest of them played games of seeing who could hurl a snowball the furthest.

"Are you sure you know where we are, Andy?" Leah asked me eventually.

"Yes, I'm just trying to find the track on the map," I said, because we'd come out on a narrow but very definite path going off to the left, which didn't appear at all. Tash and I put our heads together and studied the map, but neither of us could see the track.

"We can't be where we thought we were," Tash concluded, though neither of us could understand how that had happened, because we'd been following the map quite carefully.

"Look, we must be up here," she went on, pointing to a completely different place on the map.

"We can't be up there. We couldn't have got it that wrong," I told her.

"But this track goes off the other one at exactly the same angle that it does on the map," said Tash.

She was right, but I still couldn't work out how we could have got it so wrong.

"OK," I said eventually. "Let's turn right here, and it should bring us back to where the sledges are hidden."

"Are you sure?" Luce asked, teeth chattering.

"No, I'm not actually, but we've got to make a decision, so this is it."

With every fibre in my body I wanted to turn left, but the map seemed to be telling me to turn right, so that's what we did. We'd only gone about ten metres in that direction when I stopped dead in my tracks. I'll never forget that moment. The others were laughing as they shuffled their boots through great mounds of bright, fluffy, new snow. Something made me look up. And there it was, about two metres above me, hanging from a thin strong branch of an old shrub that had been uprooted and was poking out, black and angular, against the soft blanket of snow. The S was turning and gleaming gently on the end of its string. I climbed up and lifted it off, then half ran, half slid back down the slope, clutching my treasure. The others were completely oblivious to all this.

"Guess what?" I said, keeping my voice deliberately low and calm, but they knew immediately, and stopped what they were doing to gather round me, waiting, eyes shining. I opened the palm of my hand to show them, and a great cheer went up as Leah gave me an enormous hug and Luce proclaimed dramatically that it was a miracle. Even Twister seemed to appreciate that this was a historic moment because he did a huge mega-twist and fell over, then jumped up looking extremely embarrassed for a dog, and barked with his back to us and his tail wagging.

Finding the S put a new spring into our step, and we

covered the ground amazingly quickly for the next thirty minutes or so until we came to a place where there was a choice of three tracks. This didn't match up with the map at all. Tash and I stared at the map, concentrating as hard as we could, and Jaimes stood behind and peered over our shoulders, while the others just looked anxious. Eventually, somebody had to say it. So I did.

"It looks like we're lost."

"Lost! But it's going to be getting dark soon," said Leah, shivering involuntarily.

There was a silence while we looked at each other. My brain was whirring frantically. I felt that I'd got us all into this mess and it was up to me to try and get us out of it.

"We've got to get back to that original track and turn left," I said. "I'm going to follow my instincts, not the map."

"Can you find your way back there?" asked Tash. "Because I'm completely lost now."

"Why don't we climb to the top of that hill," suggested Fen, "then maybe we'll get a better overall idea of the landscape?"

"It's so quiet everywhere," Leah said, staring round.

I'd been feeling the stillness for ages, but it was only now that it was beginning to get to me. A few at a time, all the other sledgers had made their way home. It felt like we were the only ones showing any signs of life for miles and miles. I patted Twister and he barked at me. I wasn't sure if that was a don't-worry-I'm-here bark, or a come-on-Andy, do-something bark.

When we thought we must be getting somewhere near the top of the hill we turned and looked back to find that actually, we were only about halfway up.

"It's nearly quarter to four," said Jaimini, eyeing her watch. There was no crisp sparkle left to the snow, just a dull heaviness.

"Come on, we mustn't get dispirited," Luce suddenly said, knitting her eyebrows together and marching determinedly on. I felt grateful to her at that moment, because however optimistic and positive you are, it's not easy to keep it up if those around you are flagging. Eventually we got to the top and realized that it hadn't helped at all, because another hill lay on the other side. After a few silent seconds staring around, Tash said, "And now we really are lost, aren't we?"

I racked my brain again while the others all stood round, looking like miserable statues in the gathering gloom. Come on Andy, think. I hunched my shoulders and put my hands in my pockets as I thought and thought. It wasn't till I'd been fiddling with something inside my pocket for quite a few seconds that I realized I was clutching what might turn out to be the answer to our problems. It was a long shot but it was our only hope. Very slowly I pulled out from my pocket Sid's glove. The others were eyeing me warily as though I'd produced a hand grenade. I took the string with the S on it from around my neck and wedged it into one of the fingers of the glove.

"Does anyone have paper and a pen?" I then asked.

Jaimini slowly handed me a pen and gave me a sort of puzzled look as though she was only going along with my apparent loss of several million brain cells because there was nothing else to be done under the circumstances. Luce managed to find a crumpled receipt in her pocket and on the back of it I wrote: "Lost in Bracken Valley. Six girls. Help."

Leah was looking over my shoulder as I was writing, and reading the note out loud to the others.

"Oh come on, you're joking!" Luce immediately said. "Twister isn't Lassie, you know."

"Luce's right," said Fen. "I mean, I know this is Sid's glove, and that Twister and Sid are old friends, but you're not seriously expecting Twister to go and find Sid from here, are you. She could be anywhere. It could take him ages."

"No, I'm not. That would be impossible. But I want him to lead us in the right direction to get out of Bracken Valley the way we came in, but as he doesn't speak English I can't explain that to him. If I give him this glove he'll understand what I want him to do and he'll lead us in the right direction at least. The note is just in case he gets too far ahead and we lose him. The S is a last resort."

I stopped talking and looked to see what the general reaction was following Fen's cynical little speech.

"Andy, you're a genius!" said Tash.

"An absolute genius!" Jaimini said.

"I now pronounce you genius of the first order!" added Luce, jumping about excitedly.

"Sorry, I should have known you would have thought it all through properly," Fen said.

"I don't know how you do it," said Leah quietly.

"I haven't done it yet," I smiled back at them. "Come on, let's go for it!"

With that I called Twister and made him sit, then I rubbed Sid's glove on his nose and said, "Go on Twister. Go find Sid! Go on!" He barked at me before racing off at a hundred miles per hour with the glove in his mouth.

"Omigod!" squeaked Luce, as she hared along behind him. "I'm going to be so fit!"

"Twister! Twister!" I yelled after a few moments, when the gap between him and us was getting too wide for comfort. "Heel!" He came to heel like a good dog, so I waited till the others had caught up, then took the glove from his mouth, rubbed it on his nose again, let him take it in his mouth once more and gave him the same command to go and find Sid. This is how we went on for nearly a mile, till Tash cried out in pain because she'd twisted her ankle. While the others were looking after her I was yelling at Twister to come back, but this time he didn't hear me. He was out of sight and I'd no idea which way he'd gone, because once again it was snowing heavily and the flakes swirled around, obscuring everything.

"We've lost him and it's all my fault," Tash said, almost in tears.

"No it isn't. It's nobody's fault," Fen reassured her. "Twister'll be back in a minute, you'll see."

But though we all kept on calling and calling, Twister didn't come back to us, and there was nothing for it but to stay put. Poor Tash could only have hobbled along, anyway. Her ankle was really throbbing.

"We're going to die of exposure," Luce announced in a voice full of doom and gloom.

"No we're not," Fen told her firmly.

"It'll be dark soon," Leah said quietly.

"Helen'll send out a search party before then," Jaimini reasoned.

"It's freezing," said Tash. "I wish I could jump up and down to keep warm."

In the end we all jumped up and down, except for Tash, who hopped. But I felt so frustrated just staying in one place. I was desperate to go and search for signs of life or clues as to where we were.

"I'm just going to go up that hill to see what's on the other side," I told the others. Nobody offered to come with me and nobody tried to stop me, so off I went, feeling better because I was on the move. When I got to the top I couldn't believe it. About twenty metres from the bottom of the hill on the other side were our sledges and plastic bags. And about fifty metres away was Twister. Someone was with him, bending over and patting him. No, not just one person. From out of the swirls of snowflakes more and more people were emerging, dark shapes against the white. I stood still for a moment, then yelled out at the top of my voice, "Sid! Sid!"

She looked up and waved with both her arms. I was too far away to tell, but I just knew she would be smiling, like me. Then all the others began to wave, too, and to talk excitedly as they made their way towards me. I turned back to Fen and the others. "It's Sid! Twister's found her!"

"You're kidding!" Fen called back.

"No, she's not!" cried Sid, appearing by my side. "Come on, it's hardly any distance from here."

And I felt a lovely warm feeling inside, because I'd done it. I'd even done it without the Strays, because I'd found the sledges and I knew the way from there. It was a wonderful moment.

"I don't know how you managed to find an S in all this snow, Andy," said Sid. "You really are incredible."

And that was an even more wonderful moment.

Leah

I'd been so afraid that we were going to have to spend hours and hours more in Bracken Valley, and I was freezing cold and really worried about Tash and her ankle. The moment that Andy called out to us that Sid was there was so wonderful. And then, when we saw all the others there as well, it was unbelievable. The Strays had turned out in full force to find us. My mind was bursting with questions, like how could Twister have managed to get to Sid so quickly? And how had she alerted the others so fast? I was dying to hear their side of the story because there was no doubt about it, they were an unusual group of people.

As we made our way over the hill to join them, I was trying to work out what it was that was different about them. Then I realized. It was the way they were all standing, each person on his or her own. They looked so much stronger and more solid like this, than they would have appeared in a group. We girls hardly said a word as we made our way over to them. Andy and Sid were chatting away, but the rest of us were content to trudge along quietly. There was something familiar about one of the people standing there in the snowflakes. I stopped and looked properly. He was looking at me, too. We smiled at each other and he started to walk towards me, so I was the one standing still. My heart was racing, my knees were getting weaker by the second, and Bracken Valley was the best place in the world because this was *the boy*, the one I'd nearly met twice. The one I'd done nothing but think about ever since our first day here.

144

"Hi," he said, as he got right up to me. "I'm Jake."

"I'm Leah," I said.

"You're not going to get whisked off anywhere, are you?" he asked with a grin.

I shook my head, and we walked along side by side as slowly as we could so we could say as much as possible in the twenty minutes we'd got to get back to the phone box where the others were congregating, waiting for us.

"You took your time," one of the boys said to Jake as we joined the group.

"Yep," said Jake.

And there's no answer to that.

Tash

It turned out that Sid had been sitting at home, thinking about Andy when she'd suddenly started to wonder whether or not Andy and all her friends would be out in Bracken Valley searching for Ss in the snow. Apparently she got anxious about us all because she knew from experience how easy it was to become completely disorientated by the snow, but she also knew what a determined kind of person Andy was. The more she thought about it, the more she worried and felt responsible. She told us that she could just picture the headlines: "Six Girls on Holiday Die of Exposure in Bracken Valley After Taking Up Challenge of Local Girl Sid Robinson."

"That's when I phoned the guest house," Sid explained to us all, as we stood round the phone box. "When I heard where you were, I got the phone chain going among the Strays, and as many of us as possible came up here to try and find you. And then, on the way, an ugly beast appeared out of the snowflakes, nearly knocked me over in his excitement, and dropped this at my feet." Sid held up her glove. "Oh, this is yours, I believe," she added, handing Andy her S. "Welcome to the Strays!" Then everybody standing round, Strays and Cafe Club, broke into applause. Andy's eyes were shining. She looked so happy, and she certainly deserved it.

"I can't believe you found that, you know," said a boy called Jake, who had stuck to Leah's side like glue ever since they'd clapped eyes on each other.

"As I'm officially in the Strays now, can I call an impromptu meeting, because I've got something I need your help with?" Andy asked.

"We'll go and stand over there, where we can't here anything," said Luce, half-jokingly.

"No, you can all be honorary members," Sid said, glancing round the Strays to check that no one minded.

"I've always wanted to be honorary!" Luce announced, as we gathered as close together as possible to hear what Andy had to say. I knew what it was going to be, and I was right. She explained in as few words as possible about Emma, the cafe incident on the first day and then about Bricko, Shal and Fay more or less terrorising Leah at the guest house. I couldn't help noticing Jake's arm creep round Leah's shoulder at this point. He *was* getting protective. I thought how good they looked together, one so blonde and one so dark.

When Andy had finished her story, the Strays said that Emma needed to be taught a lesson and to leave it with them and they would deal with it. I saw Sid and Andy whispering together and I supposed they were making plans.

Mum and Auntie Alice both came along to collect us. They were filled with alarm at the thought of the danger we might have been in, and they were so grateful to the Strays (who they thought were just a group of local friends) that they insisted on everyone coming back to the guest house. There followed a big ferrying process. Jules and Auntie Alice's cars were driven backwards and forwards, backwards and forwards, picking up an endless stream of boys and girls.

My ankle was much better by the time we were all at home in front of the log fire, and it was brilliant fun to hear other stories of adventures that had happened in Bracken Valley. Andy was once again declared a hero, but she wouldn't accept it because she hadn't been able to find the track on the map. Then Sid looked at Jules's map and said, "No wonder you couldn't find it. It's not here. This map is quite an old one and that's why the track isn't marked." Andy seemed genuinely relieved to hear that. She always thinks she's failed if she does even the tiniest thing wrong.

Much later, when Sid and the others had all gone, we got changed into our pyjamas and sat round the fire eating sausage rolls and playing the game where you make up stories by adding one sentence each. It was a hilarious two hours that will probably stay in my mind for ages. Every so often Luce would jump up and pull back the curtain to peer into the darkness outside.

"Snowing again," was her first announcement, because it had stopped shortly after we'd got back to the guest house. "Lovely big flakes," was her next observation. "Sky's emptying fast. Flakes like golf balls," she said the next time, and then for her final offering, "Wouldn't it be good if snow was purple sherbet?"

"Yes, Luce," we all said, trying to keep our faces straight.

Chapter 12

Jaimini

"Let's go to ve hot wall," Peta said, clutching my hand and jumping up and down in front of me the following morning after breakfast.

"What hot wall?" asked Fen.

"Ve hot wall what talks of course, silly-billy Fenny Penny."

"What *is* she on about?" Tash asked.

We all stopped our igloo-making, partly because we'd been hard at it since half past eight and partly, I suppose, because talking walls sounded quite interesting.

"We came across this wall," Luce began.

"Yeah? And let me guess, it was hot and it talked," chimed in Fen.

"Well yeah," said Luce, and went straight back to work.

"Yes, you mentioned this before, but we didn't really take much notice at the time, did we?" Leah said, frowning at the memory.

"Oh, come on, you can't leave it there. Why was it hot? How did it talk?" Fen wanted to know.

"It hadn't got a mouf, silly-billy Fenny Penny," said Peta, standing in a very adult position with one leg crossed over the other at the ankles, and her hands on her hips. We couldn't help laughing.

"So how did it talk then?" Leah asked Peta.

"How did ve wall talk, Janey?" Peta whispered to me, behind her hand.

"Through the grille," I whispered back.

"Frough ve bill," Peta told Leah, in her most grown-up voice. "Cos his name is Bill, see?"

"What *is* she talking about?" Tash asked for the second time.

"Well, when we went off on our own the other day, to another part of the town that we hadn't seen before—" I began the sensible version of events.

"We came across a hot, talking wall," Luce finished off abruptly. "How many more times have we got to tell you?"

"How many more times, you old silly-billys?" echoed Peta, still standing in her adult pose, wearing a very adult expression to match her body language.

"Come on Jaimini, put us out of our misery," pleaded Fen, so I gave the true version of the facts without any interruptions, because I spoke very quickly. The moment I'd finished there were great cries of "I want to see it", "Let's go now", "Show us this famous wall, then", etc etc, and it didn't take us long to decide that an expedition to the hot wall would be a good idea, so we scribbled a note for Helen and left it on the door, then got the buggy and off we went.

Peta sang all the way to the wall. It was a song called "The Wall Is Called Bill", and every single line of the lyrics was the same as this ingenious title. I'm not really taking the mickey out of Peta. We all agree that for a little girl of only just three she's very bright.

As we drew nearer to the wall I began to worry in case it turned out to be cold. The others would be disappointed, Peta would *not* be happy, and Luce and I would lose a lot of cred. My fears were groundless. The wall was beautifully hot and we all snuggled up to it while Peta crouched down and shouted through the grating, "Mornin' Bill!"

We stayed silent, even though we were dying to crack up, but nothing happened. There was no reply.

"Sounds like Bill's on strike," commented Fen, giving me a withering look.

"Let's go and look round the front of the hotel, then come back. There may be someone there by then," Luce suggested, so off we trooped.

The front of the hotel was beautiful. It looked so grand and stylish, built into the crescent. Even though it was only morning, there were lights twinkling in every room, and we could even see chandeliers on in one big room downstairs. The sun had come out and the sky was bright blue in places, and mottled blue and silver in others. Leah had her camera with her and took photos for all of us, then we went round the back again.

Even as were approaching the hot bit of wall we could hear voices, which made us speed up to get there before whoever it was finished talking. It was good to see the looks on Leah, Tash and Fen's faces. They were a mixture of amused and impressed. But something was happening to the look on Tash's face. She was frowning, and as Peta opened her mouth, with the air of someone filling their lungs to sing a big number at the Albert Hall, Tash bent down and clamped her hand over it.

"Ssh, I want to listen," she whispered. We all bent down, and after a moment, each one of us wore the same frown as

Tash. There were two voices coming from behind the grate: one male, one female.

"And if you go to the other side of this wall, you'll find it's quite hot to the touch," the man was saying.

"Really!" said the woman, which made us all exchange glances, and Peta's eyes widen.

"Yes, and the other interesting feature of this wall is that from outside, passers-by can clearly hear what is being said in here."

"Oh right, I'd better watch my language then," the woman said with a giggle. And that's when we were certain about what we all now thought, which Tash had been the first to suss. The voice belonged to Helen.

Before we could stop her, Peta had put her mouth right up against the grating and said, "Hello Mummy. What you doin' in vere?"

There was a silence on the other side of the wall, and then Helen's voice sounded, but she was talking to one of the men.

"I don't understand. That sounds like my little girl."

"Cuckoo, Mummy!" came Peta's little singsong voice.

"We're on the other side of the wall," Tash called. "What are you doing in there, Mum?"

"What are *you* doing out there?" Helen said, then her voice dropped. "That's my other daughter," she explained to whoever was with her.

"Well, do invite them in," said the man.

"Yes, I suppose it does seem rather ridiculous holding a conversation through a wall," we heard Helen say.

"Come round to reception," said the man.

"Are you sure? There are seven of us," Tash said.

"No problem," the man's voice assured us, so we all

trooped round to the front, and Leah filled Andy in on what was happening on the way.

"Can I help you?" asked the receptionist, looking down her nose at us. I suppose we did look rather scruffy and damp to be standing in the foyer of a posh hotel.

"We're waiting for—"

I never finished the sentence because Helen appeared with a man in a suit. The man looked pretty important, and the receptionist obviously thought so too, because she stood up very straight all of a sudden.

"These are my guests, thank you Mrs Chamberlaine," said the man.

"It's *him*," hissed Luce into my left ear.

She was right. This was the man whom we'd seen Helen with outside the theatre, and now here they were again, only this time he was almost unrecognizable, all dressed up in a black suit. Maybe he was the head waiter or something.

"This is Andrew Faulkener." Helen introduced him in a soft voice. She didn't exactly look embarrassed, just a bit ill at ease. "This is Tash, and this is Peta," she continued, while the rest of us stood around like lemons. "And these are Tash's friends," Helen finished off.

"Well, don't tell me all their names, whatever you do," said Andrew Faulkener, smiling round at us. "I'd never remember them in a month of Sundays." Unlike Helen, he sounded perfectly relaxed. "If anybody's hungry, I'd be delighted if you'd all like to be my guests for lunch."

"Oh no, Andrew. That's very kind of you, but we couldn't possibly intrude."

"Is it buggers, Andoo?" asked Peta, which made Tash's hand shoot to her mouth as her eyes widened in alarm. The rest of us couldn't help the odd snigger escaping.

"*Burgers*, Peta. *Burgers*," stressed Helen, then she turned to Andrew with a very apologetic look on her face. Andrew, however, was having even more of a job than we were at concealing his amusement.

"I'm sure we can rustle up a burger for you Peta," he told her, recovering quickly.

"No, but the girls aren't really dressed. . ." Helen tried again, but I think Andrew saw the disappointed looks we were all beginning to assume.

"They all look fine," he assured Helen.

"D'you want to be my new daddy?" Peta then asked Andrew, which made Helen and Tash both go bright red.

"I think she likes you," Fen said to Andrew, and that somehow relaxed the atmosphere and everybody just about managed to laugh.

"Three-year-olds!" said Helen softly, raising her eyes to the ceiling in despair.

"Unfortunately, I'm already an *old* daddy," Andrew calmly told Peta.

"Have you got ketchup?" Peta then asked.

"I certainly have," said Andrew.

"Cos I like ketchup on my buggers," Peta blithely went on as she grabbed Andrew's hand and started leading him off somewhere, just as though she was in charge.

"*Burgers! Burgers*, Peta!" said Helen, but she was talking to thin air, because Peta was engrossed in letting Andrew take her to the restaurant, while the receptionist was giggling into the visitors' book and trying to look as though she had been politely minding her own business all that time and hadn't heard a single word.

"Who is he?" Tash whispered to Helen as we followed Andrew and Peta, deliberately falling back a little.

"Just someone I met. Do you like him?" asked Helen.

"He seems nice," Tash replied. "What's his job?"

"He's the manager of this hotel."

"The manager!" exclaimed six voices at once, including mine. There was a short pause then Tash asked her mum something that I'd been wondering, too. "What are you going to do when we go back home?"

"I expect we'll keep in touch," Helen answered simply.

Helen looked so pretty. It wasn't surprising that she had no trouble coming across men who liked her. Luce and I were talking about Helen a while ago and we both agreed that whenever she met a new man, it must be quite nerve-racking for Tash, in case her mum fell for someone that Tash really couldn't stand. Tash once told us that she knew her mum would never marry a man unless all the family were happy about it. So that shows that Helen's also very thoughtful, as well as being pretty. But then I already knew that about her.

Fen

At lunchtime at Brandon Hall Hotel, I was sitting next to Andy. "We're going to try and get your watch back today," she suddenly said.

"Yeah?" She'd certainly surprised me. "How?"

"I don't know. All I know is that on my own there'd be practically no chance at all, but with the Strays, we could be lucky. Do you want to come to that cafe with me, Fen? Nobody knows us in there and I want to take a look at the famous Emma."

I felt quite flattered that she wanted me to be there too,

because normally Andy would do this kind of thing on her own. I knew it was a pathetic thing to say, but I just had to be sure that she really did want me to come too, and that she wasn't simply being kind.

"I don't mind if you want to go on your own," I said.

"No, I can't do it on my own. I need you to come with me," she answered, and then I really *did* feel flattered.

So at four o'clock that afternoon, Andy and I were sitting at a table in the corner of the cafe from where we could see the whole room and all that was going on. The others had given us a good description of Emma, so we knew which one she was immediately. It was she who took our order. We noted where the tip jar was, too, then we just sat and observed, but not too obviously. We didn't want Emma to suspect we were watching her. Her behaviour was definitely rather furtive, though. She always seemed to be looking round as though there was a collection of ghosts wandering round the cafe that nobody but she could see. We knew from experience that normally, when you're waitressing in a cafe, you have to keep yourself one hundred per cent focused on what you're doing, otherwise things can easily go wrong.

"Have you noticed anything?" Andy suddenly said. I glanced round. "Don't make it too obvious, Fen."

"What kind of thing?" I asked in a whisper, because I hadn't a clue what she was talking about.

"Strays," she mouthed back to me.

I left it a moment before having another subtle look. "Where?"

"All over the place."

This whole conversation took place in the softest whisper and I began to wonder if I'd heard Andy wrongly. Maybe she'd said "trays". There were certainly plenty of those around. But I couldn't see any possible Strays among the other customers. They weren't the right age group, for a start. Most of the people in the cafe seemed quite elderly.

I must have been looking very puzzled because Andy wrote on a napkin, "In disguise". I read it, and then, as my eyes widened, she picked up the napkin, blew her nose on it and stuffed it up her sleeve. I couldn't resist another glance round, and I saw then that Andy was right. An old lady with glasses, a headscarf and very round shoulders gave me a wink and I realized it was Sid. It was all I could do not to giggle. I thought I must have been being thick but I couldn't actually work out why they were in disguise at all, until I looked at Emma. Her eyes were darting round more than ever, and I realized that she had clicked that something was wrong. She had probably sussed that the cafe contained various people who were not what they first seemed to be. And that would make anyone nervous. Whether or not Emma knew that these were Strays, I wasn't sure.

Sid suddenly called her over, saying "Excuse me" in a quavery voice, and Emma approached Sid's table cautiously, looking anxious, notepad at the ready. Andy and I had our ears flapping as hard as we could to try and hear what was being said. It wasn't difficult because there was very little conversation going on in the cafe as the rest of the Strays were sitting on their own or in twos. "Yes, could I order something please, dear?" Sid went on in the same quavery voice.

"Yes, certainly," came Emma's nervous reply. Her face looked very pale.

"I'd like one watch please," Sid said, looking Emma in the eye. At that very moment I realized that Emma was actually wearing my watch. I couldn't help gasping and that made Emma look in my direction. Her eyes were flashing with fear.

"Tut tut!" said an old man from the next table. "Fancy that!" Emma's eyes flew to the old man and she must have realized at exactly the same moment that I did that this was another enemy in disguise.

"Dear me, aren't there a lot of us?" said another male voice. "Far too many for Fay, Shal and Bricko, don't you think?"

And at that point Emma pulled the watch roughly from her wrist as though she couldn't tear it off fast enough, letting it drop on to Sid's table before rushing off into the kitchen. Sid rose slowly and, as she did so, several people got up from tables around about. Everything that had taken place up till that point had been so discreet that the manageress and the other waitress hadn't noticed anything amiss. However, with people getting up to leave the cafe *en masse*, they could hardly fail to notice. The manageress, who had been serving drinks at another table, looked startled and tentatively approached Sid.

"Is everything all right, madam?" she asked.

"No, I'm afraid that waitress was rather rude, so we're taking our custom elsewhere," she said in the most brilliant imitation of a dissatisfied old lady. She was bending down slowly to pick up a shopping bag as she spoke, because there was no way she'd get away with the disguise, despite all her heavy make-up, if anyone saw her close up. I noticed that the others were keeping their faces averted too, and relying on their body language. But there was no doubt about it, Sid was the actress of the group and she was putting on a tremendous show.

"Oh, I'm sorry, madam," said the manageress, looking completely out of her depth. Sid then came over to our table, discreetly pressed the watch into my hand, winked at Andy and touched her arm while saying goodbye to us in her old crackly voice as though we were a couple of young friends of hers. Then she slowly left the cafe with the rest of the Strays bumbling and doddering behind her. I felt like standing up and applauding loudly and I knew Luce would have been very impressed indeed.

"I still don't understand why they went to all that trouble though," I said to Andy a few minutes later.

"For two reasons," said Andy. "One, they don't want people knowing who they are, and two, all they wanted to do was to scare Emma. It's such a clever way of doing things. You see, it's all done in public, so there's no shouting, no fighting, no confrontation of any sort, in fact. They simply shock Emma into giving the watch back, at the same time making it quite clear that they're a much stronger force than Emma's friends, so presumably Emma will realize that there's no point in trying to get back at them because she'll only suffer if she does."

I was impressed. Very. The Strays were out to fight crime and to help people in trouble, and they did it all without anyone knowing who they were, a bit like a young people's SAS. Incredible!

Chapter 13

Luce

Everyone was happy. Fen had got her watch back, Helen had got her relationship with Andrew Faulkener out in the open, Andy was delighted to belong to the Strays, and Leah had apparently met the boy of her dreams! She was trying to give us all the impression that it was love at first sight, but it was pretty obvious to even the thickest of us that they must have met before. I mean, you don't just fall for someone in the middle of a snowstorm, when you're freezing cold and half-crazed with worry about getting lost never to be seen again, do you? Jaimini and I were just happy, because, well hey, why not? And Tash . . . Come to think of it, Tash was very thoughtful. It wasn't that she was miserable or anything like that, just that she seemed rather preoccupied. I wondered if anyone else had noticed that. I'm usually the last person to notice things, but this time I had the feeling that maybe I was the first. Wonders will never cease!

We went ice-skating that evening. Helen and Peta stayed at the guest house but Jules came with us. It was really fantastic. We'd all been before. I'm not showing off or anything, but I'm afraid Yours Truly was definitely the best.

The trick is to be very confident. Fen was pretty good, too, though, because of her ballet. You'd think that Andy would be the best, but it's not really her thing. It's too smooth for her.

Anyway, the moment I got the chance, I asked Tash if she wanted a break, because I wanted to test my theory (the one about Tash being preoccupied). Tash said she wouldn't mind, so we sat down together with a couple of lemonades and I eventually plucked up the courage to ask her if everything was all right.

"It's just those bumps I heard."

"You're not still worrying about that, are you? We found out what it was, after all."

"Yes, but there's still one thing I don't understand."

I waited.

"That manageress in the cafe. Don't you remember what she said on the first day?"

"Yes, that's a point." I agreed. "She said she wouldn't like to stay in the guest house because of things that go bump in the night."

"Exactly. And that couldn't have meant Peta, could it?" She was right. It was very puzzling. "I'm going to listen again tonight."

"Yeah, me too," I quickly said. Nothing was going to keep me out of this mystery! "I could go and check out what Peta's up to."

So it was agreed. I stayed awake until Jaimes was asleep, then I crept into Fen and Tash's room and snuggled down in bed with Fen, but she said I was too wriggly, so she got in with Tash and I had her bed to myself. We then kept ourselves awake by taking it in turns to think of TV personalities beginning with every single letter of the alphabet. The next thing we knew, we were all woken by a huge thud.

"What's that?" said Tash, sitting bolt upright in bed.

"What are you doing in my room?" I said, trying to open my eyes.

"Ssh, listen. See if there's anything else."

There was. Peta burst into passionate tears, then we hear Helen's soothing voice very faintly through the wall.

"Hang on a sec," I said, going over to the window and pulling back the curtain. "It's morning. Oh no, we must all have fallen asleep, and that great big thud was Peta falling out of bed." I turned round and looked sorrowfully at Tash and Fen, but they looked so funny squashed into the same bed that I burst out laughing.

"Ha ha!" said Fen in an extremely sarcastic tone. "It's ridiculous to have gone to all that trouble only to fall asleep. *And* I haven't even had my own bed."

"We'll have to try again tonight," I suggested. But Tash reminded me that this was the last day of the year. Tonight we were going to a big New Year's Eve party at the Brandon Hall Hotel, courtesy of Mr Andrew Faulkener, which meant that we would be up very late, and probably too tired to stay awake. On the other hand, maybe we could just not bother to go to sleep at all. Brilliant idea!

That day we all trooped to the shops to see if we could find anything we could possibly wear at the party. Leah was already fixed up because she'd brought a long skirt with her, and she had a really nice black top to go with it. Jaimini had got a top, but wanted a long skirt to go with it. Fen and Andy had both brought trousers that were smart enough for a party, but they wanted to get new tops, and Tash and I wanted to buy a whole outfit each. Unfortunately there was one slight problem – neither of us had very much money, but we reckoned that we might be able to stretch to a short dress each. The plan was to investigate the Oxfam shop and two other charity shops that we'd spotted. I used to think it was pointless going into second-hand shops, but actually I've realized that you can sometimes find exactly what you want in there. I proved it once again that day by managing to find a sparkling jacket that I just knew would be perfect for the party. I also found some very tight black trousers and a tiny little sleeveless top. I'd have to breathe in for the entire evening, but so what, at six pounds fifty for the whole lot, I'd breathe in for a fortnight. Talk about the bargain of the century. I'm just so lucky.

I don't know if Fen was just being kind thinking that Tash would be embarrassed if she was the only one to be wearing a short dress, but she suddenly decided that maybe her trousers weren't smart enough after all, so, like Tash, she was going to look for a short dress. There weren't any nice dresses in the Oxfam shop so we went on to the next charity shop, and there Tash found the perfect dress. It was black and white and it fitted brilliantly. Helen had some shoes that Tash really liked, and she said she could borrow them.

In the last charity shop Jaimini found a short dress. It was dark green and she looked beautiful in it. She already had some shoes that would go with it, so Fen decided to go back to her trousers idea, which proved that I was right: she *was* just being kind, making sure that Tash wouldn't be the only one wearing a dress. I'm getting extremely perceptive these days, and my vocabulary's getting bigger, too! Andy and Fen both managed to find beautiful brand-new tops in a "proper" shop(!) so we were all kitted out and ready to go to the ball.

Getting ready for the party was so exciting. We started about two hours before it was really necessary. We burned joss sticks and played loud music. The music was my idea and the joss sticks were Jaimes's. Peta went from one room to the next and bounced about happily. She called it dancing, but to anybody watching it was bouncing. Twister had decided to accompany Peta on this exercise, so while Peta bounced, he twisted. It was one of the funniest things I'd seen in my life.

The arrangements for the party were as follows: Helen was getting ready for the party at the hotel because she was going to put Peta to bed in one of the hotel bedrooms, then stay there for the night. There was an intercom in the bedroom, which meant that any one of us only had to lift up one of the phones that were dotted about all over the place and dial her room number to hear whether or not Peta was making any noise. We were going to the hotel by taxi, because Helen didn't want us walking in the dark. I think Helen was neurotic about letting us out of her sight after the episode in Bracken Valley. Anyway, it was starting to snow again, so we would have got wet feet.

At the end of the party we were all going to be picked up by Jules and a friend of hers in two separate cars and taken back to the guest house. We had no idea at what time this would be: just whenever Jules and her friend decided to leave their own party, which was being held at Auntie Alice's house. Apparently the friend would be driving right past the guest house and said she didn't mind having three girls in the car with her. Jules thought it would be at about one o'clock.

By the time eight o'clock came, we were all bursting with excitement. We'd been ready for ages. Peta and Helen had long since gone off to the hotel, and we couldn't wait to join them. We'd all put on make-up except Andy. Leah only wore a tiny bit, but then she'd look lovely even if she painted her face white! How dare she be so beautiful. I had curled my eyelashes and painted my nails. I was also proud to be wearing the biggest pair of earrings you've ever seen in your life. I did get fed up with everyone kidding me that my ears would start hanging round my shoulders, though. I had to sulk for at least ten minutes before anyone apologized and said they'd only been joking. Leah then said that "Luce wouldn't be Luce without her outrageous accessories", and I nearly threw another wobbly, but frankly, I couldn't be bothered.

We were very nearly the first arrivals at the party. Even Helen hadn't come down from putting Peta to bed. Andrew was there to greet us, though, and he stayed with us for a couple of minutes, chatting and introducing us to the few people who had already arrived. I really liked Andrew. He was about fifty, which is quite a few years older than Helen, and even rather too old for me(!) but he was nice-looking and very kind.

I couldn't work out whether the party was a private one just for people Andrew wanted to invite, or whether it was a hotel party for which anyone could buy a ticket. Either way, we felt very honoured to have been allowed to come at the last minute. There was the most magnificent buffet set out on long trellis tables along two walls of the ballroom. There was also a band and a disco. Andrew had explained that the band was playing until just after midnight and then the disco would start.

Gradually the ballroom began to fill up with guests of all ages, from about our age to very old indeed. There were some beautiful-looking women there, and I loved watching them moving about and socializing. I can't wait till I'm old enough to stroll about being cool. It was after nine o'clock when Helen came in. We all just gasped. She didn't see us at first. She was standing in the doorway looking a bit unsure of herself as she faced a roomful of people she didn't know. We were right at the other end, and I think she was probably looking for us, but then she must have caught sight of Andrew, because her eyes lit up. We saw the expression on Andrew's face, too: he looked as though he thought she was the most beautiful woman in the world. I'm not sure about that, but I was sure about one thing: she *was* the best-looking woman at that party. If I'd been Tash I would have been absolutely bursting with pride.

Helen's dress was sleeveless and went down to just above her knees. It was dark blue, very simple and plain, and hugged her figure. Her dark hair looked shiny and wonderful, and she'd put on some make-up, which I'd never seen her wear before. She also wore a necklace with sapphires, or something similar.

"She looks stunning," I breathed, and Tash just looked gobsmacked. "Andrew thinks so too," I continued. "He's got good taste, like me."

"I don't expect he sees Helen in quite the same light as you do, Luce," said Jaimini. Then we all made our way over to her and showered her with compliments, which just made her smile and say "thank you" lots of times.

"Did Peta go to sleep all right?" asked Tash. Helen said that it had taken a while but eventually she'd dropped off. Then Andrew whisked Helen off to dance because, by then, the band were in full swing and lots of people had started dancing.

They were a very clever band and were able to play all sorts of music. There was one male and one female singer, and someone on drums, along with two guitars and a keyboard, and they used all sorts of combinations of their instruments, according to what the song was. The songs were a lovely mixture too, so there was something to please everyone.

There were two boys there who I could have sworn had been among all those Strays who had rescued us in Bracken Valley. I had to admit that I couldn't recall them being at the guest house afterwards, but then maybe they didn't come back with us. They could have walked off on their own. The more I looked at them, the more I felt sure I could visualize them covered in snow, with big hoods on. I was dying to ask them if they were members of the Strays, but of course, you're not allowed to, are you? I mean, it's a secret organization and all that, so I thought that maybe I could approach them with a sort of wink and say, "Haven't I seen you somewhere before?" Then they'd instantly click on that I was a friend of Andy's and, with any luck, one of them would ask me to dance.

The boys were looking pretty spare, clutching their glasses of punch and standing about like a couple of store detectives. I thought they'd probably find it quite a relief to be approached by someone human and witty like me.

"Haven't I seen you somewhere before? I said, in what I hoped was a meaningful voice, as I winked and grinned at them.

The looked at each other as though I was a total crackpot, then one of them said in a very posh accent, "We're nephews of Mr Faulkener. We came up from Boughton Monchelsea this afternoon. Who are you?"

"Um, Luce Edmunson. I'm his niece from Cableden." The boy who hadn't spoken sniggered into his punch and I felt so embarrassed about my huge gaffe that I pretended someone was trying to attract my attention across the room, waved vigorously at the far wall and beat a hasty retreat. As I walked back to the others with my face all red, I saw that they were with a group of people, laughing and joking. Then, getting nearer, I realized that quite a few of the cast from the pantomime had turned up, including Rick, so I had to turn straight back round again, find some loos, run my hands under the cold tap till they were freezing, put them on my cheeks to cool myself down, then run my icy fingers under the hot tap to warm them up again before rejoining the party. What a performance.

It was only just after that happened that Leah and Andy both had the most brilliant surprise, because who should walk in but Sid and Jake. Apparently Helen had arranged this surprise specially. She and Jules had realized how friendly Andy was with Sid when all the Strays were back at the guest house, and they hadn't been able to fail to notice that Jake and Leah were totally wrapped up in each other, so she'd got Jules to discreetly find out where Sid lived, and from that she was able to look up the telephone number, then she'd secretly phoned Sid and invited her and Jake to the party. Helen really is a star. There aren't many mothers who'd be that perceptive.

Tash

I felt so proud of Mum when she first appeared. I didn't think I'd ever seen her looking so lovely and so happy. She and Andrew danced and danced and it was obvious they were more than just friends. I felt sort of happy and sort of worried. I worry whenever there's a man in Mum's life, because I never know if it's going to turn into something more permanent, and also you can never be sure how my brother, Danny, is going to react.

At the first opportunity Mum sought me out and asked me if I was having a good time. I said I thought the party was brilliant, because it was. She asked me if I liked Andrew, and I said he seemed very nice.

"Is he like a boyfriend, Mum?"

"We'll keep in touch and see what happens. That's all," Mum replied, which was the perfect answer. At that point Andrew came to reclaim Mum so I went to find the others.

We'd decided to try and meet as many people as possible, so we'd been taking it in turns to make the first approach to all sorts. It was a fascinating thing to do because grown-ups don't expect thirteen-year-old girls to take the initiative and go and introduce themselves. Everyone we spoke to wanted to know all about us, which made us feel very important. We'd met a group of fourteen- and fifteen-year-olds who were the sons and daughters of one or two of the guests, and they were quite nice, so we all danced together in one big group. It was Luce who had first introduced herself to a couple of lonely-looking boys, but then she'd gone bright red and disappeared from the room for ages, for some unknown reason. When we all met those boys, we found that one of them was very posh and condescending, but the other one was quite nice. Then the big surprise of the evening came when Sid and Jake walked in. The look in Leah's eyes was something to behold (to use a favourite expression of Mum's). And Andy and Sid talked and talked, which I know was very unusual for Andy, but I gather was fairly unusual for Sid, too.

The food was delicious. Luce wanted to sample absolutely everything, and then she started pretending that she was on television doing a cookery programme, to the amusement of Rick and the others. At one point Rick and Luce had a dance together. It was a rock 'n' roll number. Luce hadn't a clue what she was doing, but Rick was flinging her about all over the place so she just went with the flow: it looked like he was throwing a rag doll about. It was so funny. I could see Fen looking on enviously though, because I bet she could have done it properly. I whispered this to Mum, and she gave me a very secretive smile and said she'd be back in a minute. When she returned she had a young man with her, who looked extremely fit. You could just tell he was an athlete or a dancer or something. It turned out that he was a dancer. He went straight up to Fen, to her utter surprise.

"Excuse me," he said to her, "but I hear from a certain Helen Johnston that you are a very good dancer, and I've been looking for someone to do some rock 'n' roll with me. Would you like to?"

Fen mumbled something about not being much good at it, because I think she was worrying about dancing with someone who obviously knew what they were doing. Anyway, they danced together, and it was absolutely fantastic. For a while everybody else stopped dancing and just watched. Fen looked like something out of the film *Grease*, she was so good, and it was obvious the man was impressed. I noticed that one or two people even took photos. I found out afterwards that he'd been on television loads of times, and had also danced in the West End in all sorts of shows. Fen was in her element, and she had four dances with him altogether.

The evening got better and better because everybody became more and more relaxed. As midnight struck the champagne flowed and we all had some. I had two glasses and felt like falling over for the next half-hour, then it kind of settled down in my stomach. Everybody tried to give everyone else a kiss, but it was impossible to remember who you'd kissed and who you hadn't. In fact, there was one sweet old man who I kissed three times because he was bumbling about on his own and didn't really get kissed very much, so I felt sorry for him. I didn't see Mum and Andrew kissing, thank goodness.

By one thirty all six of us were feeling really tired. I think it was the champagne. We'd also had a glass of punch each and though we were assured there was very little alcohol in it, when you're not used to alcohol at all, it affects you much more. We were quite relieved when we saw Jules trying to attract our attention from the door. I said goodbye to Mum from all of us, and we all thanked Andrew very much indeed for a wonderful party, then he thanked me for having such a lovely mother. I didn't really know what to say to that. Leah was sad about leaving Jake, but one good thing they'd found out was that Jake's grandparents live only fifteen miles from Cableden, so at least he and Leah knew that they'd be able to see more of each other after our holiday was over.

"Do you want to listen for bumps again?" Luce whispered

to me when we were all back in the guest house with Jules.

"OK," I answered, because I'd been thinking about that on the way back in the car, and it had made me feel wide awake all of a sudden. So we gathered everyone together and told them what we were doing. It was really exciting to have another adventure in store after the party, otherwise we would all have felt depressed because of the party being over. As it was, we assembled in mine and Fen's room and got ready to listen. I was really hoping like mad that we'd hear something tonight, and it turned out that we were in luck, because we'd hardly shut the door when the tapping began. It electrified us all and we stood there, staring at each other, with wide eyes.

"It's not Peta this time. We know that," said Leah.

"Where's it coming from?" I whispered.

We all concentrated very hard on trying to work out exactly where the taps were coming from. Everything was exactly the same as the last time we'd listened. There were eight taps, then nine, then nothing.

"Could it possibly be the pipes?" Jaimini asked. "Hot water pipes do make a lot of noise, you know."

I didn't answer, just frowned. We all knew that this was not water pipes.

"I think it's coming from up here," Luce said, as she stood on a chair clutching a wooden coat hanger and gently knocking it on the ceiling in the exact place where the taps seemed to be coming from. They stopped instantly, which made us all break into nervous giggles. We waited till they started again, and then, several taps later, we tapped back with the coat hanger. Again they stopped.

"Are you scared?" Leah asked me.

"No, funnily enough I'm not," I replied.

171

"No, me neither. I would be normally, but I'm feeling good and brave tonight."

"That's because of Jake," Luce told Leah in a wise tone, but the rest of us agreed that we all felt the same.

"I think it's got to be a ghost, you know," Luce said, eyes rolling round in what she probably thought was a mysterious way, but which actually made her look rather manic.

"Yeah, yeah, yeah," said Fen, in a long-suffering voice.

"I agree with Luce," Andy suddenly said quietly, and that made us all stop in our tracks.

"Thank you, Andy," said Luce pointedly.

"Why?" Fen asked Andy.

"I don't know, really. It just seems like the only answer. Why shouldn't there be a ghost in this old house?"

"We could always ask it," Leah said, wide-eyed.

"Good idea," Andy answered calmly, then she looked up at the ceiling, while the rest of us clutched each other as though in fear of a thunderbolt striking us dead at any moment. "Are you a ghost? Tap once for yes and twice for no." The silence was so long that the excitement began to fizzle out, then a single tap made us freeze. Andy was the only one who remained calm. "Are you a friendly ghost? Tap twice for yes, and once for no." Again there was a pause and then two taps clearly sounded. "There you are," said Andy. "I rest my case." She smiled round at us all, as though she'd just looked up a word in a dictionary and been proved right about its meaning.

"Andy, how can you be so calm?" Luce asked, putting into words what we were all wondering.

"Well, look at it from the poor old ghost's point of view, tapping away, trying to attract people's attention, and nobody taking a blind bit of notice of it except to scream and be terrified. How would you like it if you always had that effect on people, and nobody wanted anything to do with you?"

I looked carefully at Andy to check she wasn't joking, but she wasn't.

"That's *it*! That's what I've been trying to say all this time." Luce suddenly said in a loud, excited voice.

"What?" I asked her.

"It wasn't saying 'Hit', it was saying 'Hi'. That's what it's been saying all the time. Eight taps for H and nine for I. It's just trying to be friendly and say 'Hi' to us!"

"So where does the T come into it then?" asked Fen.

"Don't you see? Tash was the only one to hear the T, and then she cut the poor ghost off. He was trying to say 'Hi Tash', but he never managed to get to the end of it."

For the first time ever, I thought Luce had "hit" the nail on the head.

"A friendly ghost. Fancy that!" I said. "And he was trying to talk to me. I can't believe how rude I was, going off to the loo in the hope that the tapping would stop when I got back, and then falling asleep mid-sentence."

I knew it was stupid, but at that moment in time I was actually feeling sorry for a ghost, so I looked up at the ceiling and said, "Happy New Year, Ghost."

There was a long pause and then four taps sounded. We couldn't believe it. There are four syllables in "Ha-ppy New Year", and that's exactly what the ghost had tapped.

We all went to bed shortly after that, but I didn't get to sleep for ages, and I bet I wasn't the only one. What a crazy, wonderful evening it had been!

Chapter 14

Jaimini

"Happy New Year *again!*" we all yelled at about nine o'clock in the morning.

It seemed strange to be waking up in the guest house with no Helen and no Peta. Jules joined us all for breakfast, and we went over the events of the previous evening yet again, with a lot of laughter and happiness. Fen told Jules how beautiful Helen had looked, which made Tash look very proud and happy. I think she sensed that everyone, including Jules, was wanting to know the answer to the six-million-dollar question.

"Mum and Andrew are going to keep in touch, Mum said," Tash told us simply.

"Brilliant," said Jules, clapping her hands together impulsively.

Next, Jules heard the amazing story of the friendly ghost. She kept on saying, "I do not believe it," her voice getting higher and higher. "Oh dear, d'you suppose he's been frightening the guests?" she said giggling. "I must remember to tell Tim and Fiona when they get back." (Tim and Fiona are the owners of the guest house, by the way.)

After that there was a great deal of reminiscing about

Luce and Rick rock 'n' rolling so badly together, then about Fen rock 'n' rolling so brilliantly while everybody stood round watching. Leah and Andy thanked Jules for her part in getting Sid and Jake to the party. They'd already thanked Helen and Andrew about a million times the previous evening. Luce and I didn't really have anything wonderful that stood out for us individually about the evening, but Andy had had her moment of glory during the week, and I knew she was excited about belonging to the Strays. She was going to keep in touch with Sid and maybe even start her own branch of the Strays in Cableden. She still wore her chain round her neck with the S pendant on it. I looked at Andy. She was eating her toast, half in a world of her own inside her head, and half listening to Luce going on about the wonderful Rick and another member of the cast called Angelo, who was Italian and very nice. He was also very talented. He'd been at the party the previous night and I'd seen him looking at me, but he didn't ask me to dance or anything, and no wonder really, because he was about twice as old as me. Still, he could have had a jokey dance, like Rick did with Luce. On the other hand, I wouldn't have enjoyed that at all, because I'm not, and never will be, an extrovert like Luce.

Come to think of it, though, I was the only one of the six of us who wouldn't have some wonderful story to tell when I went back. Andy would probably keep her story to herself, because that was her style, but that wasn't the point. The fact remained that she had had an incredibly adventurous holiday, Leah had met a gorgeous boy, Luce had gained recognition from a whole theatre company, especially the leading man, Tash had practically got her Mum married off to a very kind, rich man and chatted with a ghost, and Fen had danced in front of an audience with a famous dancer. Then there was little me. What had I done? Nothing. Who'd noticed me? Nobody.

Oh stop it, Jaimini, I told myself. I'd had a lovely holiday, so it didn't matter that I didn't have any personal dramatic news of any kind, did it?

"Ooh, what's this?" said Tash, who had gone to the loo and was coming back to the breakfast table holding a little white card. "It's for you, Fen."

Fen took it and gaped at it incredulously.

"What is it?" we all squealed excitedly.

"Adrian Asprey," Fen read out with a frown, then she flipped the card over.

"Please don't vanish without leaving your home address. Would like to help on the dancing front. Phone me."

"Oh Fen, it's that bloke from last night – the one you danced with. He must have been really impressed to take the trouble to come round here and drop his card in," Tash said. "And all because he thought you were so good. He wants to help you on the road to fame, Fen."

We were all grinning at Fen and the idea was slowly dawning on her. Her face broke into a big smile. Then she danced all round the breakfast room while the rest of us sang the tune of the Can-Can. Goodness knows why we were singing that. She wasn't even dancing the Can-Can. Eventually we began to calm down, and Jules said she wondered when Helen would be back.

"Oh, that sounds like her now," said Fen. There was certainly someone knocking at the door.

"No, that'll be Jake for me," joked Leah, in a very theatrical voice, while posing like one of the ugly sisters waiting for the prince.

"No, it'll be Rick for me," Luce took up the joke, draping one arm over Leah's shoulder and putting on the same ridiculous expression. The rest of us were falling about laughing, they looked so funny, especially Leah, because we weren't used to seeing this extrovert side to her.

Fen had flung open the door and stood back dramatically, thinking it was Helen and Peta. But it wasn't. Luce and Leah's dramatic poses kind of wilted, and the rest of us just stared. On the doorstep stood Angelo.

"I wasn't sure whether to knock in case you were all still in bed," he began, smiling round at us a bit uncertainly.

"No, we're wide awake," said Luce, lunging forward and dragging the poor bloke into the house. "Come in. Is Rick here?" She was peering out into the street as though Rick might be hiding in a doorway further down the road.

"No, no. No chance. Rick won't emerge till twelve o'clock."

"Twelve o'clock! I thought you had a show at two thirty? That's cutting it a bit fine, isn't it?" said Luce, as though she was the director of the pantomime, and was pulling the cast up sharply for their slovenly ways and lazy attitude.

Angelo smiled. "It's about the show that I've come, actually," he said. "You see, I've just had a call from the producer to say that the girl who played the part of Buttons's daughter has got a temperature of thirty-nine, and there's no way she's going to be able to come in for the show this afternoon."

I saw Luce's eyes lighting up and thought how lucky she was. She was about to be offered a role in the same panto as Rick. We could all feel it coming. Angelo carried on.

"The reason the producer phoned me is because I once mentioned that my stepsister – also Italian – is very dark and pretty with the right kind of poise and presence for that role. Only Sophia is staying in Wales until school starts, so that was no good. But then I suddenly had a brilliant burst of inspiration, and I said to the producer, 'Don't you worry. Just leave it with me. I know the very girl who would be absolutely perfect in that role,' and fortunately there are only two or three lines to learn. The rest is just following Buttons around really."

"Yes?" said Jules, who was as gripped and excited as the rest of us.

"So, can you do it, Jaimini?"

"*Me?*" I managed to squeak.

"Yes, of course, you." He was smiling at me encouragingly and my insides were cartwheeling.

"Oh Jaimes, you lucky, lucky, ever-so-extraordinarily-unbelievably-incredibly-lucky person!" said Luce, clutching a cushion and casting her eyes to the ceiling. "Oh why, why, *why* am I not dark and poised and pretty? Tell me that, God? Is this some kind of conspiracy? Am I destined for a life of comedy?"

By this time everybody else was practically rolling around on the floor in hysterics at the antics of Luce. But Angelo was quietly looking at me and waiting for my answer. "Well?" he asked me gently, with another of his encouraging smiles.

"OK," I whispered, wondering if this could really be happening to unimportant little me.

"Oh Jaimes, Jaimes, you're going to do it. You'll be wonderful!" cried Luce, then she turned to Angelo. "She's my best friend, you know. I taught her everything she knows."

This brought on another bout of laughter, and then we settled down, and Angelo said he needed some quiet time on his own with me to take me through the part on the stage. As though in a dream, I got my coat and went out through the front door, then got into Angelo's car. Jules insisted on driving along behind because she was suddenly panicking in case I was being abducted under her very nose. "I know I'm being ridiculous," she said to Angelo, "but you've got to see it from my point of view. I'm in charge until Helen gets back, and I'd hate to have to greet her with the news that she'd be making the return journey minus one at the end of her week away."

Luce came with Jules, and when we got to the theatre, she had a quick look inside before Jules dragged her away, saying that I would manage perfectly well without her help, thank you very much.

So there I was, on a theatre stage, learning a role. I *must* have been dreaming. Buttons was a very sweet man. He was fat and jolly and he made me relax. The assistant director was there, telling me what to do and say, and Angelo stayed in the audience watching the rehearsal. Every so often he gave me an encouraging nod or a thumbs-up sign, which boosted my confidence enormously. Then after a bit, when the assistant producer and Buttons had both said some very nice things to encourage me, I found that I was quite enjoying myself after all.

About an hour and a half later I felt prepared. Angelo came up on to the stage and said I looked lovely and that the audience would adore me. He also told me that he thought it was fate that the other girl was ill, because apparently the previous evening at the party, he'd been looking at me and thinking how perfect I would be for the role of Buttons's daughter. I felt overjoyed when he said that to me. I still couldn't believe what was happening. I must have been the happiest girl in Derbyshire at that moment.

At two thirty on the dot, the curtain rose on the stage. There were no spare seats but I knew that Helen and Peta and the others had been allowed to stand at the back, as it was what the director called an exceptional set of circumstances. "You're not kidding," I thought, when he said that.

I was nervous, but only the excited sort of nervousness. There was adrenaline rushing round my body, but I surprised myself because I couldn't wait to step on to that stage. When I did, I heard a lady in the front row say, "Ooh, isn't that young girl stunning, Dorothy," to her neighbour. After that I don't really remember much. I had to concentrate hard because I didn't want anything to go wrong because of me. I knew I wouldn't forget my lines. In fact, I thought I'd probably remember them in forty years time because I'd made so sure that I was word-perfect. But it was where to go and how to look while I was standing still with nothing to do that was the difficult part. You know that people may be looking at you even though you're not actually speaking, so you have to appear to be involved the whole time, and that is the exhausting bit. I kept on wanting to let my eyes roam to the back of the theatre to see if I could see Luce and the others, but I resisted the temptation.

By the end of the show I was hot, exhausted and elated. The audience clapped and clapped. Buttons and I had our own special bow together. When we'd bowed, he kissed me, and the audience cheered and whistled. Then we took our place in the front row of actors and actresses all holding hands. It was unreal. I did let myself look to the back at this point, and there were Luce and the others all clapping, their hands above their heads.

In the end, Buttons put his hands up to quieten the audience, and when it was all silent he said, "I just want you all to know that Jaimini. . ." He gestured at me, and my heart did a back flip because I didn't think I could take any more praise, I felt so honoured and loved. "Jaimini rehearsed this role in an hour and a half this morning, because the girl who usually plays the part is ill." He had taken another breath and was going to carry on, but the audience interrupted by clapping, so he couldn't. Then they were stamping too, and cheering, and finally – and this gave me the feeling that I wanted to burst into tears of happiness, but I couldn't – they all stood up. I was overwhelmed and had to lean into Buttons for support. He gripped me tight, and said, "You deserve it. You were superb." I wished Mum and Dad could have been there at that moment. I couldn't wait to tell them all about it.

After the show, the others came backstage and we had what was almost another party with all the cast. It was as though nobody wanted the day to end, least of all me. There was no performance scheduled for the evening that day, so the next performance would be the following evening.

I thought Luce was bearing up remarkably well and I gave her lots of hugs and kept telling her how nice she was. That's the lovely thing about Luce. I bet loads of best friends would have been sulky and jealous if their friend had the chance to do the very thing that they would have given their right arm to be able to do. But Luce was just pleased for me. It was true that she did make a few comments like, "My moment will come, just you wait," but they were all said in very good humour. I think she went up even more in Rick's estimation, though I don't suppose Luce realized that. He gave her a friendly punch on the arm and said, "You're not a bad kid really, are you?"

"What's this 'kid' rubbish?" Luce protested indignantly. "I'm an actress."

Loads of photos were taken, and apparently someone had been videoing the show as well, which made me feel over the moon, because now Mum and Dad *would* be able to see it.

Fen

What a panto! What a day! What a week!

Adrian, the dancer who had left me his card, showed up backstage at the end of the show, and we spent ages talking to each other. I gave him my address and phone number and he said he would give me some tickets to the show that he was about to be in, in London.

This, for me, was the icing on the cake, if you take it that the cake was the week's holiday. I couldn't wait to tell Mum and Dad about everything.

Tash

I can't believe we're going tomorrow. It's been a fabulous week. I really like Andrew. Mum seems so happy. When she and Peta came home, we were all treated to a blow-by-blow account of what happens in a hotel kitchen at breakfast time by Peta. Of course, as she's only just three, she's not able to express herself all that well. Consequently, we were all left with the impression that though there weren't any "buggers" for breakfast, there was plenty of "poke-ated" (perculated) coffee, or if you wanted you could have it "in the cafe", which Mum translated as decaf. You could have boiled eggs, fried eggs or "armpit" (omelette). The juices were apparently flavoured, apple, orange or "egg-sock foots" (exotic fruits). We were then given a demonstration of the speed at which the waiters and waitresses had to go in order to keep up. This involved Peta rushing round the breakfast room with her hands sticking out at the front and her bottom sticking out at the back. She fell over three times, which was the funniest part of it all. For her encore she treated us to an imitation of the head chef addressing the other chefs, for which Peta stood with her legs wide apart, her hands on her hips and an extremely grumpy expression on her face.

"Due fink I can wait all day, you lazy old fingies, cos I fink you've all got your fingers stuck!"

"He told them to pull their fingers out, at one point," Mum explained, in a rather tired, dreamy voice.

And that's how Mum stayed all the way home. Tired and dreamy. She *had* got it bad.

Leah

On the last day, Andy and I told Helen that we were going out for a quick walk, and Helen said that was fine. Quite honestly, she was in such a dreamy mood that even if we'd said we were just off on a quick trip to Jupiter, Helen would have said that that was fine, too.

"It's been brilliant, hasn't it Andy?"

"Uh-huh," she smiled, linking her arm through mine.

"Are you going to be sad to go?"

"No, not really."

"Me neither, but I feel kind of different. I feel as though something's happened to me."

"You've got tougher, haven't you?" Andy said. And I think she may have hit the nail on the head.

183

"Yes, I haven't worried half as much as I would normally, and I've really enjoyed absolutely everything. And meeting take was best of all." Andy didn't say anything, so I asked her what *her* favourite bit had been.

"I'm not sure. Maybe it was hearing Tash saying 'Happy New Year' to a ghost, and then hearing the reply!"

I laughed like mad, but Andy just smiled and I got the feeling that she'd just said that because she wasn't prepared to tell even me what her best bit really was. Andy's like that. Not exactly secretive, just a bit more private than most people. And I wouldn't have her any other way. After a bit, I got cold, but Andy said she was going for a jog and she'd be back in about an hour. I bet I knew where she was going, but I didn't question her and I could tell she was grateful for that.

Andy

When Leah had asked me what my best moment had been I'd said that it was the moment when Tash had wished the ghost Happy New Year. That was one of my best moments, but my very best moment was finding the S. I was so intrigued by the Strays and wanted so badly to pass the test and be accepted by them, yet all the time we'd been in Bracken Valley, I'd found it harder and harder to keep my positive thinking going.

After Leah went back to the house, I jogged to the park and there they all were, playing football. They stopped when I appeared and all crowded round to chat. They seemed so different from when I'd interrupted their meeting, but I realized that it was only the eerie shadows and the fact that they'd been sitting in a silent circle that had seemed kind of spooky. Thinking about it, the silence had probably been because they'd heard the approach of a stranger. And now I was one of them.

"Is Leah with you?" Jake immediately asked me, and when I told him she was heading back towards the guest house, he set off at about a hundred miles per hour to try and catch her up. The rest of us talked about Emma and what had happened in the cafe, and we all agreed that she'd certainly had her come-uppance. Then I joined in their football game for a little while before saying goodbye to all of them and giving Sid a big hug. I felt a small stab of sadness as I walked away, especially looking back and seeing everyone back in the game except Sid, who was standing on the sidelines kicking thoughtfully at the turf. But I knew I wouldn't be sad for long. I wouldn't let myself, because life goes on. Everything moves forward, and that's how I like it.

Luce

Good old Jaimini. What a goal. Fancy cracking a role in the pantomime. I'd like to tell you that I really didn't mind a bit, and that I was far too busy being happy for my best friend to give myself even the teensiest of thoughts, but that would be lying. The truth was that I was eaten up with jealousy, and wanted to scratch her eyes out. No, not really. I'm not that horrible. At least, I don't think I am. It's obvious to the most short-sighted person in the world that the resemblance between me and the girl who played the part of Buttons's daughter was roughly similar to the resemblance between Peta and John Travolta, so I couldn't really be jealous of Jaimes, could I? Anyway, she deserved a bit of attention for a change. Also, I had to admit, she looked knockout fantabulous at that party, not that she realized that. Oh, to be modest!

To try and kill my burning desire to be a fly on the wall at the rehearsal, I went to see Auntie Alice. I'd hardly seen her at all during the week, so I was able to gush on and on about how much we'd all love to come again sometime soon, and the next time I really *would* see much more of her. She was a perfectly nice person, but the week had been so action-packed that there hadn't been time for lengthy sessions of getting to know Terry's stepsister, having never met her before in my life.

Meeting Rick had been the highlight of my week. I had the feeling I would be seeing much more of him. I also had the feeling that all six of us had been touched in some fateful way by our week in Derbyshire. In fact, let's face it, a week in New York would have been a real drag compared to this, wouldn't it?

Well, that's my story, anyway, and I'm sticking to it. See ya.